THE
MARS
PROJECT

CHANGING UNIVERSE III

Also available in this series by Terrance Dicks:
SS WORLD
ECO CRASH

THE
MARS
PROJECT

Terrance Dicks

Piccadilly Press • London

CHANGING UNIVERSE III

Typeset from author's disc by Textype
in 11.5pt ACaslon Regular

Printed and bound in Great Britain by
WBC Book Manufacturers, Bridgend
for the publishers Piccadilly Press Ltd,
5 Castle Road, London NW1 8PR

A catalogue record for this book is available from
the British Library

ISBNs: 1 85340 579 5 (trade paperback)
1 85340 584 1(hardback)

1 3 5 7 9 10 8 6 4 2

Terrance Dicks lives in North London.
He has written many books for Piccadilly Press including
THE UNEXPLAINED series, the CHRONICLES OF A COMPUTER
GAME ADDICT series, the HARVEY series and THE GOOD, THE BAD
AND THE GHASTLY series.

Cover design by Louise Millar

PROLOGUE

THE SHADOWY chamber lay buried deep beneath the planet.

Vast and cavernous, it held a bank of strangely-shaped scientific apparatus.

Close by stood a long stone coffin.

Nothing had moved in the chamber for millions of years.

It was the place of the Watcher.

A needle quivered.

A low alarm chime sounded.

The lid of the stone coffin slid slowly back.

An arm emerged, long and green and skeletally thin.

Slowly, very slowly, the creature climbed out of the coffin.

It stalked across the chamber and studied the apparatus with great glowing green eyes. It reached out a long, claw-like finger and adjusted delicate controls.

The evidence was undeniable.

After millions of years there was new energy on Mars.

And energy was life . . .

WELCOME TO MARS

THE BANNER on the far side of the dusty compound read: 'Welcome to Mars'.

Tom and Sarah stared at it, hardly able to believe their eyes.

They certainly weren't back on Earth – but could they really be on Mars?

Even after all their recent amazing adventures it scarcely seemed possible.

Tom and Sarah Martin were cousins, though they'd been brought up as brother and sister. They came from Earth in the year 2015 – an Earth which had been made happy, prosperous and pollution-free by the invention of the instantaneous matter transmission system – transmat for short.

Tom and Sarah had been making a routine transmat trip from New York back home to London when something had gone wrong. They'd found themselves in a world where the Nazis had won World War Two, and Britain was under the brutal dictatorship of the Nazi SS.

They'd escaped from the SS world only to find themselves in yet another parallel world, one where the Emperor Napoleon had won the war between England and France, and his statue, not Nelson's, was on top of the column in Trafalgar Square.

Their stay in the Napoleonic world had been brief.

Suddenly they found themselves in a polluted world where civilisation had collapsed, the climate ruined by global warming.

After surviving such perils as murderous bandits and giant mutated rats they'd escaped – only to find themselves here!

They'd been prepared to find themselves in another universe – but not on another planet!

An amplified voice boomed, 'You two! Get over here – move!'

'Now what?' whispered Sarah. 'We're not really on Mars, are we?'

Tom shrugged. 'Only one way to find out!'

They moved forward . . . As they walked across the compound, Tom and Sarah glanced curiously about them, taking in their strange new surroundings.

Behind them was a long row of transmat booths, including the one from which they'd emerged.

Ahead of them lay a huge open area. It was surrounded with high metallic walls, but open to the sky above. It was a strange-looking sky, reddish rather than blue.

'Why does walking feel so weird?' asked Tom.

They felt incredibly light, seeming almost to float across the ground.

'Lower gravity,' said Sarah. 'You weigh less than half what you did on Earth.'

'Well, I suppose it's one way to lose weight!'

The air was hot and dry and somehow thin, lacking in oxygen. It was as though they were on top of a mountain.

'How come we can breathe out here in the open?' asked Tom. 'I thought there was no atmosphere on Mars?'

Sarah shrugged. 'There is now!'

On the other side of the compound was a long reception counter, divided into sections. Queues of people stood before each section, talking to uniformed officials, then gradually filtering through a series of gateways behind the long counter, and disappearing into a dome-shaped building beyond.

Tom and Sarah joined the shortest queue and waited. There were only a couple of people ahead of them. Soon they found themselves standing opposite a sharp-faced man in a neat grey uniform.

'Names?'

'Tom Martin,' said Tom.

'Sarah Martin,' said Sarah.

'Brother and sister?'

'Cousins,' said Tom. 'Sarah's mother was my mother's sister and she married my father's brother.'

'Never mind the family history,' said the man in a bored voice. He studied his computer screen and said flatly, 'No.'

'No what?' asked Tom.

'You're not here.'

'Yes we are,' said Sarah. 'Large as life! If you could be bothered to look away from that screen you'd actually see us!'

'You're not here on screen, on my list,' said the man, as if that was all that mattered.

'Well we're still here,' said Tom. 'Where do we go now?'

'Down to miscellaneous,' said the man. 'Far end.' He jerked a thumb to his left.

'Thank you so much for all your help,' said Sarah through gritted teeth. 'Pity you can't manage a little common courtesy to go with it.'

The man looked at her in amazement. He obviously wasn't used to people answering back.

Tom grabbed her arm and led her away. 'We've only just got here,' he said. 'Let's not start any fights yet!'

'Miscellaneous' was a smaller section than the others, with a sad-looking little man sitting behind the counter. He looked up as Tom and Sarah appeared.

'Hullo,' he said as they approached. 'My name's Reg. Can I help you?'

'Thank goodness,' said Sarah. 'A human being at last!'

'Gave you a hard time, did they?' asked Reg sympathetically. 'They're under a lot of pressure right now.'

'And you're not?' asked Tom.

'I just take care of the odds and ends,' said Reg.

'That's us all right,' said Sarah.

Reg grinned. 'What's up, then?'

'They say we're not on the list.'

'Can't see how that happened. This is the first batch of colonists, all hand-picked volunteers.'

'We're not supposed to be here at all, really,' said Tom.

'You volunteered for the Mars Project, didn't you?'

'No we didn't,' said Sarah.

'So how come you're here?'

Sarah shot Tom an appealing look. She'd spoken without thinking – before they'd had time to work out what they were going to say.

Tom thought fast. 'We arrived by accident,' he said.

'What sort of accident?'

'A transmat malfunction.'

'Transmat never malfunctions!'

'That's what you think!' said Tom. 'We were transmatting from New York to London. Somehow we ended up here.'

It was more or less true − if you left out a couple of side-trips to alternative universes on the way!

Reg frowned. 'That's impossible. The terrestrial and interplanetary systems are completely separate.'

'They must have got mixed up,' said Sarah. 'Or we wouldn't be here.'

'So we'd like to get back to Earth as soon as possible, please,' said Tom firmly.

He looked quickly at Sarah and she gave him a brief nod.

As so often happened, the cousins were in unspoken agreement.

Whatever kind of alternative universe they'd arrived in, they stood a better chance of getting home to their universe from a parallel version of Earth than from a remote colony on Mars.

Reg scratched his head. 'Well, this is a new one! I'll have to make out a special report. The Administrator will want to see you. It may take a while, she's got a lot on just now.'

'So what do we do meanwhile?' asked Tom.

By now everyone had passed through the reception area and the compound was deserted.

Reg thought for a moment. 'I'll give you temporary passes and you can join the others. At least you'll get something to eat and a place to sleep while you're waiting. Names?'

He took their names and stood them in front of a little screen. The machine whirred and produced plastic badges bearing their names, their photographs and the words 'NEW COLONIST'.

'Self-adhesive,' explained Reg. 'Put them on and go through there. I'll put in that special report right away. Good luck!'

Tom and Sarah stuck on their badges and went through the gate. It led into a long corridor, where bored officials handed out sets of one-piece coveralls in some light silvery material. There were changing rooms on each side of the hall.

Tom and Sarah changed, and emerged to admire each other.

'What do you think?' asked Sarah.

'Neat but not gaudy,' said Tom. 'What do *you* think?'

'Well, it's not exactly a fashion statement, is it?' said Sarah. 'Still, it'll have to do.'

They went on into a big dome, which had obviously been designed to receive huge numbers of people. There were rows and rows of seats and a raised platform with a screen behind it at the far end.

The little group of recently-arrived colonists, some fifty in all, was occupying rows of seats, just below the platform. They were being addressed by a tall, white-haired woman in a blue uniform. Other blue-uniformed officials stood around her.

When Tom and Sarah appeared the tall woman called, 'Come along, you two, you're late. We've already started.'

Tom and Sarah came forward and found seats at the rear of the little group.

'Like being late for school assembly,' whispered Sarah as they sat down. 'Come to think of it, she looks just like my old headmistress!'

'As I was saying,' said the tall woman, 'you are the first colonists to enter the Mars Project. You are a small group, but many more will follow you. A few minor difficulties have delayed the opening of the colonisation programme. We are confident that the immigration programme will soon be in full swing. Meanwhile, here is the introductory film which will begin your stay on Mars.'

The officials moved aside and the screen lit up.

The film which followed was a documentary about the colonisation of Mars.

It began with the first steps in terraforming, the process by which the first pioneer scientists transformed Mars into a planet on which human beings could live.

It showed the construction and installation of the giant orbital mirrors which focussed the sun's rays and melted the planet's polar ice caps, thus providing carbon dioxide.

Asteroids of solid ice were moved to the planet from the nearby asteroid belt to provide water vapour. More water vapour came from the melting of the layer of permafrost below the Martian surface. The combination of water vapour and carbon dioxide provided the beginning of an atmosphere.

Then the newly-formed atmosphere was seeded with millions of tons of blue-green algae. Through photosynthesis, the algae produced oxygen – and the beginnings of a breathable atmosphere.

The process of turning Mars into another Earth had begun.

It had taken fifty years.

Now the early stages were over, and the process of colonisation was about to begin.

Sarah, who was something of a science buff, watched in fascination. Tom's interests lay more in Earth's past and he found the film heavy going. What's more, it was so obviously propaganda. He felt there was something fake about it. Everything was just too good to be true.

The film showed the development of the Mars/Earth transmat link, the one thing that made the whole process possible.

The first pioneers had arrived on Mars by rocket-ship, over fifty years ago. One of their early experiments had been the setting up of a transmat link with Earth. Nobody really expected it to work – but it did.

Although colossal amounts of power were required, interplanetary transmat really worked. With transmat in operation, equipment, supplies and personnel could be transported quickly and easily from Earth to Mars.

Now, according to the commentary, the Mars colony was on the brink of a wonderful future. Computer-simulated pictures showed happy, prosperous colonists working on farms, building cities and relaxing in beautiful exotic parks and gardens.

The film finished with a surge of inspiring music and the screen went blank. Sarah turned to Tom. 'It's amazing, isn't it?'

Tom nodded, not wanting to spoil her pleasure. 'I never realised transmat could work between planets.'

'Why not? We know it works between alternate worlds! Transmat science must be far more advanced in this universe,' Sarah went on. 'Maybe their scientists can figure out a way to get us back home.'

'Maybe,' said Tom. 'The thing is, what's going wrong here on Mars?'

'What do you mean?'

'You heard what that headmistress-type said, up on the platform. "A few minor difficulties." '

'So?'

'One thing you can rely on in any universe,' said Tom. 'When a public official tells you there are a few minor difficulties, that means you're in real trouble!'

'What do you think is the matter, then?'

'I don't know – but something is! I can feel it. Somehow things on Mars just aren't as wonderful as they're trying to make us believe.'

As if to reinforce Tom's words, a strange figure suddenly appeared on the platform. It was a bulky, white-bearded old man, wrapped in a ragged cloak.

'Showing you their little propaganda movie, are they?' boomed the old man. 'Don't you believe a word of it. If you've got any sense, you'll all transmat straight back to Earth. The Mars colony hasn't got a chance. You're all doomed!'

CHAPTER TWO

THE PROFESSOR

BLACK-UNIFORMED security guards hurried on to the platform and tried to bustle the old man away.

He brushed them aside.

'All right, all right, I'm going. I just wanted to let these poor devils know what they're in for. Someone ought to do it!'

There was a buzz of excited chatter amongst the group of colonists.

'It looks as if you were right,' said Sarah. 'There *is* some kind of trouble here. I wonder what that was all about?'

'I don't know,' said Tom. 'Here comes someone who might.'

The tall, headmistressy woman had come down from the platform. She was crossing the hall, followed by a group of assistants.

Tom and Sarah jumped up from their seats and went over to intercept her.

'Excuse me,' said Tom.

'Not now, young man,' said one of the assistants. 'Can't you see the Administrator is busy?'

'I just wanted to ask a question,' persisted Tom.

The Administrator stopped and looked at him in haughty amazement. Like the first clerk at the desk, she seemed astounded that a mere colonist would dare to speak up.

'Well?'

'I wondered what that business on the platform was about.'

'Don't worry about it,' said the Administrator dismissively. 'It's really none of your concern.'

It was exactly the tone Sarah couldn't stand. 'I'd say it was very much our concern,' she said sharply.

'Really?' replied the Administrator freezingly.

'Yes, really,' said Tom. 'You show us a film telling us how wonderful everything's going to be, then some whiskery old codger pops up and says we're all doomed.'

There was a murmur of agreement from the other colonists.

'That's right,' said a tired-looking man. 'Why don't you answer the kid?'

The Administrator looked as if she was about to make an angry reply. Then one of her assistants whispered in her ear – clearly reminding her of the importance of public relations.

She turned back to Tom and Sarah with an insincere smile.

'Forgive me if I was abrupt, there's so much to be done – especially now, when our first draft of colonists has just arrived. There's really no need to worry.'

'That's quite all right,' said Tom. 'No need to apologise.'

'But you still haven't answered our question,' said Sarah.

Tom and Sarah stood there, looking at her expectantly.

The tall woman sighed. 'The gentleman on the platform is Professor Muldoon,' she said. 'As you see, he's getting on in years. Unfortunately, his mental balance isn't all it should be. Occasionally there are these unfortunate outbursts . . .'

'If he's ill, why don't you have him looked after?' asked Sarah bluntly.

'Professor Muldoon is one of the oldest and most respected people on Mars. He actually landed here with the first astronauts, over fifty years ago. He helped to set up the first Mars base, worked on the early stages of terraforming . . .'

'What's the matter with him, then?' asked Tom. 'If he's such a pioneer, why is he making all this fuss?'

The Administrator looked sad. 'We're rather afraid

that all the early hardships affected his brain. He's prey to all kinds of strange fears and worries. Recently he wandered off into the desert and was lost for several days. It seems to have made things worse.'

'Shouldn't he be sent back to Earth to be properly cared for?' asked Sarah.

'Perhaps he should,' said the Administrator. 'But he would never agree to go. Professor Muldoon has given his life to the service of the Mars colony. It would be cruel to send him back to Earth. So, we humour him, and try to put up with his little outbursts.'

'Thank you for explaining,' said Tom politely.

Really she hadn't explained much at all, he thought, but it was obviously all he was going to get.

The Administrator looked at him curiously. 'What's your name, young man?'

'Tom Martin. This is my cousin Sarah Martin.'

'And what made you decide to be Mars colonists? You're both very young – and you don't seem quite the usual type.'

'We didn't,' said Tom.

'Didn't what?'

'Decide to be colonists.'

'Then why are you here?'

'We're here by mistake,' said Sarah. 'A transmat mix-up. Reg on the gate is writing a special report about us.'

'We'll have to look into it,' said the Administrator.

'But meanwhile, since you are here – do try to fit in!'

She marched away, followed by her assistants.

'That sounded rather like a threat, didn't it?' said Tom thoughtfully.

'What did she mean, about our not being the usual type?'

'Look around you,' said Tom.

Sarah looked. Most of the colonists were older than they were. Their faces were careworn as if their lives had been difficult.

'I see what you mean. They look as if they've had a hard time.'

'Perhaps they have,' said Tom. 'I don't suppose you'd volunteer to come and colonise Mars unless things on Earth were pretty bad.'

'You got that right,' said the tired-looking man standing next to them. 'No jobs anywhere unless you've got a string of degrees.' He held out his hand. 'Name's Chad.'

Tom and Sarah shook hands and introduced themselves.

'Things were pretty tough for you all before you came?' asked Sarah sympathetically.

'I'll say,' said a woman nearby. 'And what with welfare being cut all the time . . .'

Other colonists joined in with a chorus of complaints. Pretty soon Tom and Sarah got a picture of the state of things on Earth in this universe. In their own universe, computerised automation had been phased in gradually, with people being retrained. But in this universe automation had raced ahead, putting millions of people out of work. With whole firms and factories being run by a computer and one or two technicians, there were jobs only for a highly-educated elite.

A huge unemployed underclass had been created, too many for the world government to support.

'This Mars colony business seems like a pretty good deal,' said Chad. 'Guaranteed jobs, food and a place to live. Plenty of people jumped at it. I hope nothing goes wrong, it's our last chance.'

An amplified voice boomed out. 'A meal is now available in the dining area, which is in the adjoining dome . . .'

Eagerly the little crowd surged forward, carrying Tom and Sarah with them.

Back in her large and impressive office, the Administrator was studying the computer print-out of a brief report. It told her very little more than she knew already. Two extra colonists had arrived shortly after the main batch. They had claimed their presence on Mars was due to a mix-up between the terrestrial and interplanetary transmat services – which was scientifically absurd.

The office door opened and a very large man in an

elegant black uniform strode into the room.

He had an impressively craggy face, a heavy, brutal jaw and close-cropped black hair.

'You wanted to see me, Administrator?'

She pushed the print-out across the desk. 'I did, Commander Ryan. I thought you ought to see this.'

Ryan read quickly through the report. 'So – someone's made us a present of two extra colonists? I wonder why?'

'They claim not to be colonists at all, that they're here by accident.'

Ryan tossed the report back on the desk. 'Rubbish! Someone sent them. The only question is who and why . . . Have you seen them?'

'I was speaking to them just now. They actually had the audacity to stop me and start asking questions.'

'Did they, indeed? What about?'

'That old fool Muldoon made a scene after the induction film.'

'We really ought to do something about him,' said Commander Ryan thoughtfully.

'Too dangerous. He's got too many powerful friends in Earth Government.'

'These two new arrivals . . . What are they like?'

'One male, one female. Both impertinent.'

'And both curious!'

'You think they're agents of some kind?'

'Almost certainly.'

'They seem very young,' said the Administrator doubtfully.

'Could be a double bluff,' said Commander Ryan. 'Instead of trying to hide your agent, you send someone so unusual they'll never be suspected.' A thought struck him. 'Or perhaps you do both.'

The Administrator looked alarmed. 'You think there are more spies, hidden amongst the colonists?'

'Almost certainly,' said Commander Ryan again. 'It will be interesting to see who these two contact. Let's have them in, shall we? I'd like to take a look at them.'

The Administrator nodded. 'And the other business?'

'Dealt with!'

'The creature's body . . . ?'

'Fed into the atomic furnace.'

'And the guard who killed it?'

'In the furnace with the creature.' Ryan smiled. 'He had an unfortunate accident soon after he told me what he'd done.'

'You dealt with everything personally? No one else knows?'

Ryan nodded his head. 'Not even my men.'

'Keep it that way,' said the Administrator. 'If Earth Government ever learn we're not alone here, they'll close this project down.'

'Putting both of us out of work, and ruining all our plans!' said Commander Ryan. 'And we can't have that now, can we? Let's take a look at our two new arrivals.'

The Administrator checked a desk chronometer. 'They'll be eating now.'

'Then I'll have them picked up when they finish.' He smiled. 'We'll try a touch of the old hard–soft treatment.'

The crowd of colonists had moved through a short tunnel into the adjoining dome. It was much like the first, except that it was set out with benches and long tables.

At the far end a curved conveyor belt appeared at one side, crossed the back of the dome, moving from left to right, and disappeared into the other side. The conveyor belt held trays covered in some silvery material.

Another conveyor belt ran beneath the first, but this one was empty.

Tom and Sarah watched as the colonists moved to the conveyor belt, grabbed the passing trays and carried them over to the tables.

'Seems straightforward enough,' said Tom. 'Let's give it a try.'

They collected a couple of trays and carried them to an empty table. There were plenty to choose from. Like the first dome, the dining area was designed for more people than were actually there. No doubt it was ready for the thousands of colonists soon to come.

Tom and Sarah lifted the hinged lids of their trays, revealing the compartments beneath. The different sections held a variety of hot food. There was soup, bread, an assortment of vegetables, some kind of stew and a container of hot tea.

Plastic eating utensils – knife, fork, spoon, cup – were fitted into the lid of the tray.

Tom and Sarah looked at each other.

'School dinners!' exclaimed Tom.

Sarah sniffed the food. 'Only not as good!'

'We'd better try it, all the same,' said Tom. 'Got to keep our strength up.'

They began to eat. The food wasn't bad, but it wasn't that good either. It looked all right, but it was curiously bland, with little real flavour.

'Processed or simulated or genetically modified or something,' said Tom. 'Imitation food!'

'Yuk!' said Sarah, pushing away her tray. She was an organic vegetarian, with occasional lapses.

'You'd better give your dietary principles a rest,' advised Tom. 'I don't think they cater for health-food freaks up here. The others don't seem to have any complaints!'

All around them the colonists were eagerly devouring the contents of their trays. Several of them had already finished their first tray, put the empty container on the lower conveyor belt, and helped themselves to a second tray.

One of them was Chad, the man who'd spoken to them in the other dome.

He gave them an apologetic grin as he carried his second tray to a nearby table. 'I know – looks a bit greedy, doesn't it?' he said. 'But when you've missed quite a few meals, you grab what you can get!'

Suddenly Sarah pointed. 'Look!'

Sitting alone at a table was the old man who'd appeared on the platform. He had taken off his cloak, revealing a set of well-worn coveralls.

Tom and Sarah looked at each other. As so often happened, they were sharing the same thoughts.

'Let's go and have a word with him,' said Tom.

They carried their trays over to the lower conveyor belt and moved over to the old man's table.

'Mind if we sit with you?' asked Sarah.

The old man looked up from under bristling white eyebrows. 'You don't want to sit with me,' he rumbled. 'I'm an outcast, I am. You'll get yourself in trouble with the authorities.'

'Blow the authorities,' said Sarah. She sat down, and Tom did the same.

'I'm Sarah Martin,' she said. 'This is my cousin Tom.'

The old man grunted.

'We know who you are,' said Sarah brightly. 'You're Professor Muldoon.'

He glared suspiciously at her. 'Know all about me, do you? I saw you talking to the Administrator. Did she send you to spy on me?'

'Don't be ridiculous, sir,' said Tom cheerfully. 'We've only just got here. We were asking her about what you said up on the platform, after the film.'

'And what did she tell you?'

'Not a lot. She suggested you were . . .'

'Barmy?' snapped Muldoon. 'Crazy? Mad?'

'Well, misguided,' said Sarah tactfully.

He glared at her with faded blue eyes. 'And what do you think?'

'I don't know what to think,' said Sarah frankly. 'But you look sane enough to me. What did you mean, about us all being doomed?'

'Why are you asking me all these questions?' snapped the old man.

'Surely that's obvious,' said Tom. 'If somebody pops up and tells you you're doomed, you're bound to take an interest!'

Professor Muldoon's lips twitched in a grim smile. 'What else did our dear Administrator tell you about me?'

'Not much,' said Sarah. 'She said you'd been lost in the desert and come back rather . . . ill.'

'I came back with the truth,' said Professor Muldoon fiercely. 'Only nobody wants to hear it.'

'We do,' said Tom.

The old man gazed into the distance. 'We're not wanted here,' he said suddenly. 'It's their planet, and they won't tolerate us.'

'Who won't?' asked Sarah.

'You'd only laugh if I told you. You'll just say I'm crazy, like all the rest of them.'

'You sound far from crazy to me,' said Tom. 'From what the Administrator says, you know more about Mars than anybody else. I've got a feeling something's very wrong here – and if anyone can tell us what's going on, it's you!'

'Maybe I can and maybe I can't,' said the old man. He broke off, a suspicious look on his face. 'I'm not sure about you two. I need to think.'

'Can we talk again?' asked Sarah.

'Maybe . . . we'll see.'

He hurried away.

Tom and Sarah looked at each other.

'Who won't tolerate us?' asked Sarah. 'He never really explained that bit, did he?'

'The Martians, I suppose.'

'But Mars is a dead planet,' said Sarah. 'Or it was before humans came along and terraformed it. There aren't any Martians!'

'Professor Muldoon seems to believe in them!'

'Yes, he does, doesn't he?' said Sarah. 'What do you think? Is he mad?'

Tom shrugged. 'Who knows? He's certainly a bit paranoid. But you know what they say . . .'

'What?'

Tom grinned. 'Just because you're paranoid, it doesn't mean they're not out to get you!'

'I think someone's out to get us right now,' said Sarah. She pointed.

Tom looked round and saw two black-uniformed security guards marching down the aisle towards them.

They stopped at the table, looking down at them.

'Tom and Sarah Martin?' barked the one in the lead.

'That's us,' said Tom.

'Come with us.'

'Why?'

'The Administrator wants to see you.'

As always, Sarah reacted badly to being bossed around.

'Suppose we don't want to see her?'

'I don't think you've got much choice,' said the security guard. 'You're under arrest.'

CHAPTER THREE

ON TRIAL

THE GUARDS marched them out of the dining area, along linking tunnels, and into a smaller dome, furnished as a large and impressively ultra-modern office.

The Administrator sat behind a massive executive desk.

I don't trust people with enormous desks, thought Tom to himself. They're usually would-be dictators!

Beside the Administrator sat a very big man with close-cropped black hair and a heavy, brutal face. His black uniform resembled that of the security guards, but it was obvious that he was of a much higher rank.

He was studying them both with keen interest, a look of mild amusement on his face.

Tom and Sarah came to a halt in front of the desk, flanked by their guards.

The Administrator gave them a frosty glare.

'So. Tom and Sarah Martin . . .'

She's trying to frighten us, thought Tom. And that baboon beside her looks as if he belongs in the Nazi SS.

Tom decided it was time to seize the initiative. He glanced quickly at Sarah – he knew he could rely on her to back him up.

'Yes, those are our names,' he said politely. 'I'm afraid you have the advantage of us.'

'What do you mean?'

'You know our names, but we don't know yours.'

The Administrator looked furious at being inter-rupted, but somehow she couldn't refuse to reply.

'Very well, if you insist. I am Doctor Audrey Becker, Administrator of the Mars colony.'

'And the gentleman next to you?'

It was the big man himself who answered. He had a deep, rumbling voice. 'I am Commander Ryan of IMCSC – the International Mining Corporation Security Corps. I am head of security for this base.'

'Thank you,' said Tom even more politely. 'You must be a busy man.'

The big man smiled. 'Things get a little hectic sometimes. But I manage to cope.'

Sarah gave him her most charming smile. 'I'm sure you do. You look very capable.'

'Too kind.'

All this chat was getting on the Administrator's

nerves. 'Perhaps we can proceed,' she said impatiently. 'You are both charged . . .'

This time it was Sarah who interrupted. 'You said *charged* . . . Is this some kind of trial?'

The Administrator frowned. 'Well, not exactly . . .'

'Because if it is a trial,' said Sarah, 'shouldn't we be informed about our rights? Aren't you going to appoint a defending counsel?'

Sarah was very big on human rights – especially her own. And surely even an alternative universe must have some kind of judicial system.

The Administrator, for her part, felt a sudden twinge of anxiety. The girl seemed very confident. In fact, they both did. If these two were agents of some kind, they might have powerful friends. It might be wise to treat them carefully.

'This isn't exactly a trial,' said the Administrator. 'It is, however, an official enquiry, and you would be well advised . . .'

'If it isn't a trial, perhaps we could have some chairs?' suggested Tom. 'It's been a long day and we're both a bit tired.'

The Administrator lost her temper. 'Stop interrupting me, both of you!'

Unexpectedly the big man smiled.

He almost looks like a friendly gorilla, thought Sarah. One who might turn very nasty at any moment!

'It's a reasonable request, Administrator,' said Commander Ryan. He looked across at the two guards. 'Chairs!'

The guards hurried to fetch two moulded plastic chairs from the side of the room.

Tom and Sarah sat down.

Sarah smiled sweetly at the Administrator. 'Now – how can we help you?'

The Administrator drew a deep breath. 'You are cha– *suspected*, that is, of spying. To be precise, of industrial espionage.'

'Why?' asked Tom.

'What?' said the Administrator, thrown yet again.

'It's a simple enough question,' said Sarah. 'Why are we suspected of spying?'

'You arrived here by some irregular means,' snapped the Administrator. 'Your names are not on the list of colonists, and your story about a transmat malfunction is scientifically impossible.'

'Maybe it is,' said Tom. 'But it happened.'

'Otherwise we wouldn't be here,' said Sarah.

Determinedly, the Administrator ploughed on. 'You began asking indiscreet questions as soon as you arrived . . .'

Tom yawned. 'Forgive me for interrupting again, but this is just silly!'

'Silly!' The Administrator was outraged.

'For a start,' said Tom, 'who are we supposed to be spying on, and why? This isn't a military installation, is it? What secrets have you got?'

'My corporation has invested heavily in the Mars Project,' said Commander Ryan. 'Rival corporations might be very interested in our progress and our problems.'

'We have political opponents too, even in Earth Government,' said the Administrator. 'Some politicians think the project is too expensive, that it should be cancelled. They would be glad to obtain information to use against us.'

'Fair enough,' said Tom. 'But I still say the idea of *us* being spies is plain silly.' He looked at Commander Ryan. 'Presumably you're a security expert, commander?'

The big man smiled. 'I suppose you might call me that.'

'What sort of person makes a good spy?'

Before Ryan could reply, Tom answered his own question. 'Someone who doesn't get noticed, blends in with the background. We haven't exactly managed that, have we?'

Commander Ryan seemed amused. 'Ah, but you're forgetting the theory of the double bluff!'

'What? Oh, I see!' Tom grinned. 'You mean sending somebody so obviously suspicious that nobody would ever believe they were really a spy?'

'Something like that, yes.'

'Well, it may be a theory,' said Tom. 'But I very much doubt that any spy would be daft enough to try it out!'

'That's right,' said Sarah. She turned to the Administrator. 'We wouldn't have been chosen for the job in the first place. You said yourself earlier, we're the wrong age and the wrong type.'

'If we *were* spies,' concluded Tom triumphantly, 'we'd look and sound exactly like all the other colonists – complete with hard-luck stories to match!'

'What about all the questions you were asking?' demanded the Administrator. 'And why were you so quick to make contact with Professor Muldoon?'

'We asked questions because we were curious,' said Sarah. 'How else are we going to learn anything?'

'And we didn't "make contact" with Professor Muldoon,' said Tom. 'We saw him in the dining area and went over to talk to him.'

'Why?'

'Because of what he'd said on the platform about our all being doomed,' said Tom. 'Something like that is bound to arouse your interest!'

'And what did he tell you?' asked Commander Ryan interestedly.

Tom shrugged. 'Not much. He seemed pretty confused.'

'He was pretty paranoid as well,' said Sarah. 'He suddenly turned on us and accused us of spying on him –

just before your two guards turned up and carted us off.'

Commander Ryan was silent, apparently thinking over what they'd said. 'I admit that you've made some good points,' he said at last. Again he gave that curiously charming smile. 'But if you're not spies, what the devil are you?'

'Exactly what we say we are,' said Sarah. 'Lost travellers. All we want to do is get home!'

'Why don't you just send us back to Earth?' suggested Tom.

Commander Ryan and the Administrator exchanged glances.

'We may very well do that,' said the Administrator. 'But I'm afraid you'll have to remain here while we make some more enquiries.'

'And what's going to happen to us right now?' asked Tom.

Commander Ryan considered for a moment. 'Strictly speaking, I ought to lock you up in a cell.'

'That's not fair,' protested Sarah. 'We haven't done anything! We didn't want to come to Mars, you know!'

Commander Ryan seemed to come to a decision. 'I think I'm going to give you the benefit of the doubt. I don't think there's enough evidence to justify locking you up as spies.'

The Administrator opened her mouth to object, but he silenced her with a look.

It was suddenly clear to Tom and Sarah who was really in charge here.

'There's no point in your joining the others, since you're not going to be colonists,' he went on. 'We'll put you in the VIP guest quarters until our enquiries are complete.'

The Administrator gave him an astonished look, but she didn't say anything.

'Meanwhile, you can have the freedom of the base,' Commander Ryan continued. 'Take a look around. Maybe you'll decide to stay and become colonists after all!'

'What happens when you've finished your enquiries?' asked Tom.

'That depends on the result of the enquiries,' said Commander Ryan. 'If you're cleared you'll be sent back to your anxious relatives on Earth with my apologies.'

'And if we're not cleared?' asked Sarah.

'Then you'll be shot,' said Commander Ryan cheerfully. 'Shall we go?'

The guest quarters turned out to be two simple but reasonably comfortable rooms, linked by a bathroom, in a nearby dome. Each room had a bed, a couple of chairs and a table. There was even a bowl of fruit and bottles of mineral water on each table.

On each bed there was a plastic travel pack, containing pyjamas and various toiletries.

Tom and Sarah sat in Tom's room having a conference.

'That was a sudden change of heart,' said Sarah. 'From spies to honoured guests in no time at all. What made them change their minds?'

Tom took a rosy red apple from the bowl, bit into it, and made a face.

'Tastes plastic . . .'

Instead of answering Sarah's question, Tom tapped his lips, then his ears, and then gestured around the room.

Sarah frowned for a moment, then nodded her understanding. He was telling her that the room was probably bugged. Better not say anything they didn't want overheard.

Tom yawned loudly. 'I suppose we may as well get some sleep. Mind if I use the shower first?'

Without waiting for a reply, he went into the bathroom and turned on the shower and the wash-basin taps.

He reappeared in the doorway and gestured to Sarah to follow him.

'What are you doing?' she whispered.

'Bugging the bugs – I hope. It works in old spy movies, anyway!'

'Why bother? We're not guilty of anything, and we're not going to say anything that proves we are.'

'Maybe not. But people can get the wrong idea, words can be twisted.'

'Then you don't think they've really changed their minds about us?'

'No, I don't. They're still suspicious, but they don't know what to make of us. They're just giving us enough rope.'

'They're what?'

'Giving us enough rope to hang ourselves,' said Tom. 'Traditional old saying.'

Sarah shuddered. 'So what do we do now?'

Tom yawned again. 'Like I said, get some sleep. Tomorrow we'll take advantage of the commander's kind offer and take a look around . . .'

Sarah nodded. 'Maybe we can sneak into their transmat and send ourselves home!'

In the Administrator's office, Commander Ryan and the Administrator sat listening in frustration to the sound of running water. The commander clicked the switch of the listening device and the sound cut off.

'I rather think they're on to us,' he said. 'They're a clever pair – too clever to say anything incriminating.'

'We should have locked them up,' insisted the Administrator.

'And what would we learn from that?'

'But to set them free, let them roam around the base wherever they like . . .'

'They're only free here on the base,' said Commander Ryan. 'Where else can they go? And they'll be watched every minute. With any luck, we'll discover what they're really after.'

'And suppose they do the discovering?' demanded the Administrator. 'You said yourself, they're a clever pair. Suppose they find out about . . .'

'Two bodies, both reduced to atomic dust? There's nothing left to find out about!'

'I don't like it. I think they're dangerous.'

'I find them rather intriguing,' said Commander Ryan. 'But I really can't believe they're much of a danger to us, not now we're on to them. As you said yourself, they're still very young.'

The Administrator refused to be reassured. 'Did you see how cool they were under questioning? They may be young, but I'm convinced they're trained agents. They might be from one of those fanatical eco-warrior student organisations.'

Suddenly a terrified-looking man in the white coveralls of a technician burst into the office.

The Administrator was outraged. 'This is a confidential conference about important security matters! How dare you interrupt . . .'

'Transmat's crashed,' said the technician. 'We've lost all contact with Earth!'

Tired as she was, Sarah found it difficult to get off to sleep. For a start the room wasn't completely dark. A dim night-light glowed in the ceiling, and there didn't seem to be any way of turning it out. She felt oddly weightless as she lay on the bed, as if she might float away. Presumably she was still adjusting to Mars gravity.

The dome's air-conditioning made the air in the room feel hot and dry. Sarah sat up and fumbled for one of the bottles of mineral water on the table.

She took a swig and was about to lie down again when she heard a distant voice. Maybe Tom was talking in his sleep.

No, there were two voices . . .

She got up and went quietly into the bathroom. The voices were louder now.

She heard Tom say, 'Look, it's no use going on at me. I've got nothing to tell you.'

She peered through the open door to Tom's room and saw that he was propped up on one elbow in bed.

Standing over him, menacing him with some kind of hand-gun, was a shadowy figure.

'For the last time,' said the intruder. 'Tell me who you are and who you're working for.'

'You already know our names,' said Tom. 'And we're not working for anybody.'

The intruder jabbed the gun towards Tom's face.

'I'm running out of patience. For the last time, tell me the truth. If you don't – well, I can't afford to take any chances. Speak up – or I'll kill you, here and now!'

THE SPY

SARAH REALISED she was still clutching the mineral water bottle. She leaped forward and hit the intruder on the head with it, as hard as she could.

Since the bottle was made of plastic she didn't do very much damage. But the distraction itself was enough.

As the man swung round, Tom sprang from the bed and wrestled him to the ground.

Sarah hovered over the struggling figures, looking for a way to help. She saw a hand clutching a gun stick out from the tangle. Quickly, she bent down and grabbed the weapon, twisting it out of the attacker's hand.

Seeing what had happened, Tom shoved the man away and got up, dragging the intruder to his feet.

Fortunately his opponent seemed to be quite a small man . . .

Suddenly Sarah realised that it was one particular

small man. It was Chad, the tired-looking little man they'd met on their arrival.

She recollected Tom's words to Commander Ryan about the sort of person who'd make a good spy. Someone who wouldn't get noticed, who'd blend in with the background. Someone who'd look and sound exactly like all the other colonists. Complete with hard-luck story . . .

In other words – Chad!

But why had he picked on them?

Tom shoved the unresisting Chad into the bathroom.

Sarah followed, covering Chad with his own gun, which seemed to be some kind of pistol. She had no idea how it worked, and she wasn't going to shoot anyone anyway. Still, as long as Chad didn't know that . . .

Turning on the wash-basin taps again, Tom looked at the silent Chad. 'Keep your voice down, we think the place is bugged. Now, it's our turn to ask the questions.'

'That's right,' hissed Sarah. She brandished the pistol and did her best to look menacing. 'Start talking!'

Chad scowled at them. 'What about?'

Tom spoke in a low voice. 'You can start by telling me why you picked on us to attack.'

'Can you wonder?' said Chad bitterly. 'You've loused things up for me completely.'

Tom was baffled. 'How? What have we done?'

'I spend months building up my cover, sleeping in doorways, doing lousy labouring jobs, always exhausted and half-starved. I manage to get myself in the first draft of colonists. Then you two turn up with the stupidest cover-story I've ever heard, start making trouble and get security all stirred up. Who are you from, one of those batty, half-baked student eco-warrior set-ups?'

'We're not from anyone or anything,' said Sarah. 'How many times must we tell you?'

Chad wasn't listening. 'Security will double-check everyone all over again now. I'll be lucky if I don't get caught myself! If you had to come here interfering, why couldn't you at least come with a half-decent cover-story?'

'It's not a cover-story, it's the truth,' said Sarah. 'Look, who are you, who do you work for?'

'Why should I tell you?'

'Because I've got the gun.'

'Gonna shoot me, are you?' sneered Chad. 'That'll take some explaining away.'

'We don't have to shoot you,' said Tom. 'We'll just call security and turn you in to Commander Ryan.'

'You wouldn't,' said Chad. But he looked uneasy.

'Why not?' snarled Sarah in her best gun-moll voice. 'We'd prove our loyalty, score a few points with Commander Ryan and it would take the heat off us!'

'If you turn me over to Ryan's thugs, they'll beat me up until I tell them all I know and then shoot me!'

'Take your choice,' said Tom. 'Talk to us, or talk to Commander Ryan.'

Chad didn't reply.

He was a tough man, not easily frightened. Sarah decided to try persuasion rather than threats. 'Listen,' she said gently. 'I don't say we're on your side — we don't even know what your side is! But we're certainly not spies ourselves, we're neutral.'

'Just tell us what's going on, and you can clear off,' said Tom. 'I give you my word on it. We won't turn you in and we'll forget all about tonight.'

After a moment Chad said, 'All right, I suppose I've got nothing to lose. If you must know I work for CPU — the Colonists Protective Union.'

'And what are you up to, here on Mars?'

'We've been getting reports that the IMC are planning to exploit the colonists on Mars for their labour — and rip up the planet as well.'

'And what are you hoping to do about it?' asked Sarah.

'I'm trying to get evidence to force Earth Government to hold a public enquiry.'

'How do the IMC fit in here on Mars, anyway?'

Chad looked at her in surprise. 'Don't you two know anything?'

'We've been travelling,' said Tom hastily. 'We're a bit out of touch.'

'The Mars Project is an enormously expensive business,' said Chad. 'Earth Government didn't want to pay for it all themselves, so they took in IMC as a sort of

48

partner. At least, that was the idea.'

'So what's gone wrong?' asked Sarah.

'From what we hear, IMC are planning to take over completely here on Mars. They want to run things to suit themselves.'

'We just got hauled up before the Administrator and Commander Ryan,' said Tom. 'Ryan certainly seemed to be the one in charge.'

'He is,' said Chad grimly. 'IMC are completely ruthless, worse than all the other multinationals put together. They're more powerful than any single country, and very nearly as powerful as the government.'

'What's in it for them?' asked Tom.

'Mining rights,' said Chad. 'Lots of valuable minerals on Mars. IMC have ripped up big chunks of the Earth already. Now the minerals are running out, and Earth Government is finally starting to regulate the multinationals.'

'And IMC think they'll have a free hand, here on Mars?'

Chad nodded. 'They've ruined most of one planet and now they're ready to start on another.'

Sarah was horrified. She was almost as keen on protecting the environment as she was on human rights.

'That's terrible! They've got to be stopped!'

'That's what I'm trying to do,' said Chad grimly. 'If you two don't spoil it for me.'

'We won't spoil things,' said Sarah. 'We'll help you! Won't we, Tom?'

'If we can,' said Tom more cautiously. 'We're not in a very good position ourselves. They're pretty suspicious of us already.'

'That's right,' said Sarah. 'But you're all right, Chad! No one seems to suspect you. While Commander Ryan thinks we're the people he's after, he won't be bothering with you!'

'So we haven't spoiled anything, we're helping you,' said Tom. 'We'll be a distraction for Ryan.'

'And he can investigate us as much as he likes because there's nothing to find,' said Sarah. She looked at Chad. 'Well, do you believe us? Or do you still think we're spies – like you?'

'Not any more,' said Chad.

Sarah looked surprised. 'What's changed your mind?'

Suddenly Chad reached out and took the gun from her hand. 'Safety's still on,' he said. 'No trained agent would ever make a mistake like that!'

'You mean the safety was on when you were threatening to kill me!' said Tom.

'Well, of course it was. These things are dangerous, I didn't want to hurt anybody!'

'You might as well have it back, I suppose,' said Tom. 'We seem to be on the same side – more or less.'

Chad put the gun away. 'Did you mean what you said – about helping?'

'Yes of course,' said Sarah. 'What can we do?'

'Just keep your eyes open. I'll have to stick with the other colonists, but you'll have a bit more freedom.'

'What are we looking for?' asked Tom.

'Anything odd or out of place. I think there's something badly wrong here – something they're trying to cover up.'

'Professor Muldoon agrees with you,' said Sarah.

'Is he the old guy who made such a fuss after the film? I noticed you talking to him after we ate. What did he have to say?'

'He said the Martians wouldn't tolerate us here,' said Sarah.

'Poor old fellow's potty,' said Chad. 'There aren't any Martians, everyone knows that now. Never were. Mars was a dead planet until we came. That's why it's so suitable for terraforming and eventual colonisation.'

'What would happen if there were any Martians still surviving?' asked Sarah.

'Earth Government would hand the planet straight back to them.' Chad laughed. 'Some of the other colonists were talking about this Muldoon. Apparently he wandered off into the desert and went off his head. So don't worry about the Martians, they don't exist.'

'Professor Muldoon thinks differently,' said Sarah.

Chad shook his head unbelievingly. 'Take it from me, it's IMC you've got to watch out for. Now, I'd better be getting back.'

With a nod of farewell he slipped out into the dimly-lit corridor.

When he'd gone Tom said, 'You were a bit hasty, weren't you, Sarah? Saying we'd help him.'

Sarah gave him an indignant look. 'We can't just stand by and let IMC ruin the planet!'

'It's not our planet,' said Tom. 'This isn't even our universe, remember. All we want to do is get home. We haven't got time to get mixed up in local politics.'

'We're mixed up anyway,' Sarah pointed out. 'Just because we're here. Anyway, if Muldoon's right, and we're doomed, we haven't got any choice.'

'How do you mean?'

'Unless we find out what's wrong here, we won't survive to go home!'

Tom yawned. 'I'm too tired to argue. Let's try to get some sleep . . .'

Commander Ryan sat by himself in the Administrator's office. He was watching a monitor screen. It showed Chad slipping silently along the corridors of the VIP suite.

Commander Ryan looked up as the Administrator came back into the office. 'Any progress on transmat?'

She shook her head despairingly. 'Complete power-loss. No transmission, no communication. We can't even send messages, let alone people – or your precious minerals, if we ever get any! I've got technical staff working non-stop, we'll just have to hope they come up with something.'

She sat down at the desk, rubbing her eyes wearily. 'I bet those damned kids have something to do with this! It can hardly be a coincidence that it happened just after they arrived.'

'They haven't had much opportunity, have they?' objected Ryan.

'They could have sabotaged something as soon as they arrived,' said the Administrator. 'Planted some device.'

Ryan smiled. 'I think it far more likely that their collaborator was responsible.'

'You've found him?'

Ryan re-ran the surveillance video. 'You see?' he said. 'I told you it was worth waiting. Now there's another one in the net!' He sighed. 'Our two charming young friends seem to be spies after all.'

'We should arrest all three at once,' said the Administrator.

Commander Ryan shook his head. 'We'll watch them a while longer. There may be others.'

'But suppose they find out . . .' She broke off. 'If word ever gets back to Earth – well, your precious corporation's mining operations will be finished for a start. They'll put an end to the whole Mars Project.' Her voice rose in sudden panic. 'I'll be out of a job. Poor and starving, back on Earth!'

'I've already told you, that isn't going to happen,' said

Ryan. 'And as for our spies – we can dispose of them any time we think it's necessary. And for the moment, it doesn't really matter what they find out, does it?'

The Administrator stared wildly at him. 'What do you mean?'

Ryan laughed. 'It's ironic, really. Whatever they find out, they can't get the information back to Earth!'

'I still say we should round them up and shoot them!'

Ryan put his hands on the Administrator's trembling shoulders. 'We've got more pressing problems to worry about than three bumbling spies. You know we can't survive here for very long, not without supplies from Earth.'

'Of course I know that!' said the Administrator hysterically.

'Well, my dear Administrator, unless those damned technicians of yours repair transmat pretty quickly, all of us – bureaucrats, spies, colonists and security men – will die right here on Mars!'

CHAPTER FIVE

DANGEROUS
KNOWLEDGE

TOM LIFTED the lid of his breakfast tray. 'Bacon and egg, porridge, toast and coffee,' he said. 'It looks all right – though what it'll taste like . . .'

Sarah was already tucking into her breakfast. 'It's not bad, actually. I think it's all made from reconstituted protein or something, but they've got the taste more or less right . . .'

The nearby tables were filled with hungry colonists. After a couple of meals and a night's sleep they all seemed less subdued, and they were chattering eagerly.

Chad carried his tray over to their table and sat down. 'Morning!' he said cheerfully. 'Sleep well?'

'Not without interruption,' said Tom.

Chad lowered his voice. 'Sorry about that!'

'What are the happy colonists doing today?' asked Sarah.

'We're starting something called a training and acclimatisation course this morning. Lasts for a couple of days. After that we get sent on to the outer bases.'

'This isn't the only base on Mars, then?'

Chad shook his head. 'This is just the reception centre and HQ. There are smaller bases all over this part of the planet.' He took a swig of his coffee. 'This isn't bad . . . What are you two doing today?'

'Whatever we like, as far as I know,' said Tom. 'Provided Commander Ryan doesn't change his mind and have us locked up.'

'Get as good a look round the base as you can,' urged Chad. 'I'll meet you here for supper and we can compare notes.'

A buzzer sounded and the colonists began finishing off their breakfasts, carrying the trays to the conveyor belt and filing out. Chad followed them, and a few minutes later Tom and Sarah did the same. They found themselves in one of the tunnel-like corridors that linked the various domes. Blue-uniformed officials were marching busily up and down. They looked curiously at the two strangers, but nobody stopped or spoke to them.

'It's weird,' said Sarah. 'They're all wondering who we are and what we're up to, but nobody says anything.'

'Typical bureaucrats,' said Tom. 'Keeping their heads down and not getting involved. They all hope we'll turn out to be somebody else's problem.'

'So what do we do now?' asked Sarah.

'That's a very good question,' said Tom. 'We won't get anywhere just wandering around at random.'

Sarah thought for a moment. 'You're right. We need help.'

She marched up to the nearest of the passing officials, a worried-looking man clutching a pile of computer print-outs.

'Excuse me?'

The man looked alarmed. 'Yes?'

'We're visitors,' said Sarah. 'Guests of Commander Ryan.'

The man looked even more worried.

'Commander Ryan suggested we take a look around the base,' said Tom. 'But it's all so big and confusing we don't know where to start.'

'We wondered if you could help us,' said Sarah. 'Or at least, put us in touch with someone who could.'

The man brightened at the prospect of passing the job on to someone else. 'Central Operations,' he said. 'They're the people you want. The nerve centre of the whole base. Come along, I'll take you there.'

Clearly anxious to be rid of them, he led them along the maze of connecting tunnels, and up to a door marked 'Restricted Area'.

There was a security guard standing outside. 'Restricted area,' he said gruffly. 'No visitors.'

Their escort waved him away. 'VIPs,' he said importantly. 'They're here to see Central Operations. Commander Ryan's orders.'

The security guard stood aside.

They went through the door into a dome filled with banks of communications equipment and rows of monitor screens.

White-uniformed technicians moved hurriedly to and fro, taking readings, checking instruments, holding low-voiced, urgent conferences.

'There you are,' said their guide. 'It's all here. They may not have much time for you now, there's some sort of flap on. Still, I'll see what I can do.'

He went over to the nearest technician, who was worriedly studying one of the monitor screens.

'VIP visitors,' he said again. 'Guests of Commander Ryan. Look after them, will you?'

He turned and hurried away, happy to have dumped his problem in someone else's lap.

The technician, however, looked far from happy. Sarah decided it was time to turn on the charm. 'I'm sorry about all this,' she said, giving him her most winning smile. 'I can see how busy you are with important work. It's not fair you should be landed with us. Only Commander Ryan said that this was the place to find out what was going on.'

'That's right,' said Tom. 'He told us it was the nerve centre of the entire base!'

'If you could spare the time to give us a very quick look round?' said Sarah.

They both looked at the technician with expressions of flattering interest.

'Well, just for a few minutes,' said the technician. He lowered his voice. 'We're having a spot of trouble with transmat – unexplained power losses. I expect it'll soon be sorted out.'

He led them amongst the banks of machines.

'These instruments monitor the progress of the terra-forming process,' he explained. 'We're boosting the amount of oxygen in the atmosphere, melting the permafrost to provide more water and convert the deserts into usable soil. The work began here, and it's boosted by the ring of sub-stations around the planet.'

'What about the mining?' asked Tom, with an air of idle curiosity. 'Is there much going on yet?'

'Only a limited amount,' said the technician. 'To be honest, it's a bit of a tricky subject.'

'Why's that?'

'The terraforming scientists are strongly opposed to mining, at least for the moment. But IMC are keen to expand their mining operations as soon as possible.'

'Why are the scientists against mining?' asked Sarah.

'They think it's too soon, they're worried it will affect the terraforming process.'

The technician led them to a map-screen, which

showed a vast area of the featureless Martian landscape.

He pointed to a large bright spot at the centre of the map. 'This is us, here . . .'

He indicated a widely spread circle of smaller light-spots around the edges of the map. 'And these are the sub-bases.'

Sarah noticed that some of the outer lights were flashing. 'What's different about the ones flashing?'

'It's an emergency signal,' said the technician. 'Several of the outer bases have suddenly started having power-loss problems as well. It's endangering the entire Mars Project.'

'Does anyone know what's causing it?'

The technician lowered his voice. 'Not for sure. Some of the scientists think it might be caused by the mining . . . Vibrations in the permafrost or something . . .'

A shrill electronic alarm sounded and another of the sub-station lights started flashing.

Technicians gathered around the screen.

'Another one,' said somebody. 'That's three in as many days. If this keeps up the terraforming will go into reverse. We'll have to leave Mars.'

'We can't leave Mars,' said another voice. 'Transmat isn't working, remember. We can't transmat to Earth, and they can't transmat to us – we can't even communicate!'

A babble of excited voices arose.

'When they don't get our routine messages they'll know something's wrong.'

'They'll send a rocket ship . . .'

'Not in time. We'd all be dead by the time it got here.'

'That's right! I bet all the bigwigs get away all right, though. They'll have special arrangements.'

Tom turned to Sarah. 'They're starting to panic.'

Sarah nodded. 'No wonder the Administrator was so worried about us being outsiders. If this gets out and the colonists panic as well . . .'

Suddenly the Administrator's angry voice cut through the babble of excited voices. 'Quiet, all of you! Get back to your posts.'

The little crowd melted away.

The Administrator glared angrily at Tom and Sarah. 'You two! I might have known. Don't move!'

She turned to the remaining technician – the one who'd been showing Tom and Sarah the map.

'I heard the alarm in my office. What's happened?'

'Another sub-station's gone down, Administrator.'

'Any details?'

'Not yet, Administrator. They'll be trying to get through on the emergency circuits now.'

'Let me have a full report as soon as anything comes through.' She turned to Tom and Sarah. 'And as for you . . .'

She called to the security guard outside the door. 'These two are under arrest. Bring them along to Commander Ryan's office.'

* * *

The commander's office was smaller than the Administrator's, but just as hi-tech. He was sitting behind a small desk, made to look even smaller by his impressive bulk.

He rose as Tom and Sarah were marched in by the guard, the Administrator close behind them.

'Ah, there you are, my young friends! I was just wondering where you'd got to.'

The Administrator turned to the guard. 'Get back to your post. And this time be more careful who you admit to a restricted area.'

When the guard had gone, she looked accusingly at Ryan. 'I can tell you exactly where your young friends had got to, commander. I found them in Central Operations – just as the news of another sub-station crash came through. You'll have to get rid of them now. They know too much . . .'

She turned and stalked out of the office.

CHAPTER SIX

ACCIDENTAL DEATH

COMMANDER RYAN shook his head.

'You two really do have a talent for getting into trouble, don't you?'

Sarah gave him a look of wide-eyed innocence. 'I've no idea what you mean, commander. What are we supposed to have done now?'

'You invited us to take a look around the base,' said Tom.

'That wasn't meant to include restricted areas! How the devil did you manage to get into Central Operations?'

'Simple,' said Sarah. 'We told one of the Administrator's staff we were your guests, he told the guard the same thing . . .'

'And the guard assumed it was all official because it came from someone on the staff?'

'That's right,' said Tom cheerfully.

Commander Ryan nodded. 'Then, no doubt, you managed to find a technician gullible enough to tell you everything you wanted to know – even though everyone had been told to keep quiet about the transmat crash.' He sighed. 'No security system ever devised is proof against human stupidity. However . . .' He looked at Tom and Sarah. 'Being in Central Operations at all is bad enough. But to be there when the news of a sub-base crash came through . . . That really is too much. I'm beginning to fear that the Administrator is right, and you'll have to go!'

He paused for a moment. 'Of course, if you were both to make a full confession . . .'

'What about?' said Sarah. 'We've got nothing to confess. We told you yesterday we aren't spies.'

'And very convincing you were, too,' said Commander Ryan. 'But that was yesterday. Today . . .'

He switched on the monitor screen and turned it round so they could see. The screen showed Chad coming out of their quarters and moving quietly away.

'The surveillance video shows him entering your quarters and then leaving a short time later. Unfortunately we have no record of your conversation. Somebody seems to have left the tap running!'

Tom and Sarah looked quickly at each other. Both were thinking hard. If they didn't come up with a convincing story . . .

'That video doesn't prove anything about us,' said

Tom. 'It only proves something about Chad – that he came to see us last night!'

Commander Ryan sat down, leaning back in his chair, which groaned beneath his weight. He seemed to be enjoying himself.

'The question is – why did he come to see you?'

'We were as puzzled as you are,' said Sarah. 'Believe it or not, he suspected us of being spies. He asked the same old questions – who were we, who were we working for . . .'

'And what did you tell him?'

'The same as we told you. We're nobody's agents, we're here by accident, and all we want is to go home.'

'And why did Chad ask you all these questions? Who is he working for?'

Sarah shot Tom a quick glance, and he nodded back. He had no intention of telling Ryan any more about Chad than was necessary. Not even to save their own skins. All the same, his options were limited. He couldn't deny the visit, as there was video evidence of it. But as for the rest . . .

'No idea. We didn't ask him and he didn't tell.'

'We even thought he might be working for you,' said Sarah. 'He was asking much the same sort of questions!'

Commander Ryan nodded thoughtfully. Did he believe them? There was no way to tell.

'And what was the end result of this interesting midnight conversation?'

Tom shrugged. 'We convinced him we were telling the truth and he went away.'

'And when you saw him at breakfast this morning?'

'He said he was sorry for disturbing us, said he was about to go on some course with the other colonists.'

Commander Ryan said, 'So your night-time conversation was completely innocent – at least as far as you were concerned?'

'That's right.'

'We have the beginning of the conversation on tape,' said Commander Ryan. 'It appears to confirm your story. It breaks off suddenly with the sounds of a struggle.'

'He was threatening Tom, so I hit him with a bottle,' said Sarah.

'Very enterprising,' said Ryan. He leaned forwards. 'If you are as innocent as you claim to be – *why did the rest of the conversation take place in the bathroom, deliberately obscured by running water? An old spy trick, by the way!*'

Tom thought hard. 'That's a very good question,' he said.

Commander Ryan smiled coldly. 'And do you have a very good answer for me?'

Tom shrugged. 'I was just being careful,' he replied. 'The tape of a conversation about spying could be made to sound bad for us. Tapes can be doctored. As for the old spy trick with the running water – I saw it in an old spy movie.'

Commander Ryan was silent for a moment. Then he said, 'It may interest you to know that I re-checked my security files and came up with an identification of this Chad. He's an agent of a militant organisation, the Colonists Protective Union. They have a fierce hatred of IMC. We have had a lot of trouble with them.'

'Never heard of them,' said Sarah. 'What's going to happen to Chad?'

'I was just about to arrest him.'

'When you do, ask him about last night. I'm sure he'll confirm our story.'

Commander Ryan rose. 'All right. Let's go and ask him.'

With any luck, Sarah's right, thought Tom to himself. We did our best to keep poor old Chad out of trouble. We can only hope he'll do the same for us.

Summoning two guards, Commander Ryan led Tom and Sarah out of his office, along a number of corridors and out into a large, open-air compound, much like the one in which they'd arrived.

The compound held a little group of colonists, shivering in the chill of the thin Martian air. They were inspecting a massive piece of machinery, rather like a colossal tractor with a bladed shovel-like device mounted on the front.

There didn't seem to be any sign of Chad.

Maybe he's escaped! thought Tom.

Sarah nudged him in the ribs. 'Look!'

Tom looked. At the edge of the compound stood Professor Muldoon. Wrapped in his cloak, leaning on his staff, he watched the colonists.

He waved to them, and Tom and Sarah waved back.

The professor came over to them. 'Good day, my young friends. Come to see the Mars colony at work?'

'That's right,' said Tom. 'Commander Ryan here insisted on giving us the full tour.'

'I'm sure you'll find it fascinating,' said Professor Muldoon. 'Perhaps the commander will permit me to explain something of what's really going on? Now take these unfortunate men here . . .' He waved his stick at the colonists. 'Lured to Mars by promises of an Earth-like paradise, they find themselves on a long-dead planet where new life is only just finding a foothold. Hoping to till the soil, grow their own crops, own their own farms, they find themselves dragooned into operating a mechanical monster which will rip the guts out of this poor old corpse of a planet. When they have worked themselves to death in the noble cause of making IMC richer than ever, more colonists will replace them, lured by exactly the same false promises.'

'You paint a gloomy picture, Professor Muldoon,' said Commander Ryan. 'No progress is achieved without suffering and self-sacrifice.'

'*Your* progress, commander,' said Professor Muldoon. 'IMC's progress.' Once again he waved his stick at the watching colonists. '*Their* suffering and self-sacrifice!'

'You have a privileged position here, professor,' said Commander Ryan coldly. 'I advise you not to abuse it, or you may find your privileges abruptly – withdrawn.'

Ignoring him, Professor Muldoon turned to Tom and Sarah. 'I've been thinking about our little chat earlier. I'd like us to talk again. There's quite a lot I'd like to tell you – about Mars – and the Martians!'

He glared defiantly at Ryan as he spoke.

'We'd be happy to talk again,' said Sarah.

'As soon as we're – at liberty,' said Tom.

'That may not be for some considerable time,' growled Commander Ryan. He rounded angrily on Professor Muldoon. 'As for you, professor, I advise you to guard your tongue – and stop upsetting my colonists with your stupid public speeches. If you don't, I'll have you arrested here and now. And don't think your powerful friends on Earth can save you. We happen to be a little out of touch with Earth Government and your powerful friends.'

'It's true, then,' said Professor Muldoon. 'Transmat really is down?'

Commander Ryan mastered his growing anger. 'Just a temporary problem. It will soon be fixed.'

'Of course,' said Professor Muldoon. 'Tell me, commander, did it ever occur to you that you might have brought your troubles on yourself? That Mars is striking back because of the way you have treated the planet?'

'Rubbish,' said Commander Ryan.

'I don't know,' said Sarah. 'There's a theory that planets are alive. Maybe the professor is right. Maybe all your troubles are simply the revenge of Mars.'

'Or the Martians,' said Tom. 'It sounds like an old sci-fi movie, *The Revenge of the Martians*.'

'Many a true word spoken in jest, my boy,' said Professor Muldoon. He raised his stick in salute and marched away.

Commander Ryan glared furiously at Tom. *'What did you mean by that?'*

Tom shrugged. 'Just a thought. Suppose there really were Martians? And suppose one of them had been injured, or even killed. By one of your men, say. The other Martians might take their revenge . . .'

'Melodramatic nonsense,' said Ryan, and turned away. He scanned the compound. 'Now, where's your friend Chad got to? He should be in that group somewhere.'

The colonists, meanwhile, were listening to an instructor who wore the white uniform of the technical staff. His raised voice carried clearly across the compound.

'This machine is your basic strip-mining equipment,' he announced. 'The scoop on the front digs deep into the desert, the filter at the rear separates out the valuable minerals. The cargo of ore is then sent back to Earth for processing. In time we shall have our own processing plants on Mars. You will all learn to handle this machine . . .'

One of the colonists shouted, 'We came here to be farmers, not miners!'

'All in good time,' said the instructor. 'Until agriculture can be established, mining is the Mars colony's main source of income. The machine is simple to operate. I will now demonstrate . . .'

He marched away and climbed into the driver's seat of the huge machine.

Slowly it rumbled forward. As it moved away it revealed a little group of colonists who'd been standing on the other side of the machine, hidden by its massive bulk.

One of them was Chad.

At the sight of Tom, Sarah, Commander Ryan and the two guards, Chad froze for a moment. Suddenly his hand went inside his coveralls, emerging with the stubby little hand-gun.

'Look out!' yelled Tom. 'Get down, Sarah!'

As they threw themselves to the ground a shot whizzed over their heads, and then another.

'Arrest him,' ordered Commander Ryan.

Drawing their weapons, the two guards set off after Chad.

Chad fired another shot at them, missed, and then turned and dashed across the compound. Looking over his shoulder as he ran he fired another shot – and stumbled straight into the path of the advancing machine, which was now gathering speed at a surprising rate.

There was one terrible scream . . .

The giant Caterpillar treads rolled over Chad's body, crushing him into the Martian dust.

Commander Ryan turned and yelled back inside the dome. 'Stretcher party! Paramedics!' He shouted at the instructor, who had frozen in shock, 'Move that machine back!'

The machine rolled back.

Men ran out of the dome and went over to the broken body.

One of them examined the body briefly, then looked up at Commander Ryan and shook his head.

They lifted Chad's body on to a stretcher, covering it with a silver blanket.

Commander Ryan turned to Tom and Sarah, who were just getting to their feet. 'A most unfortunate accident. Now there's nobody left alive to confirm your story . . .'

CHAPTER SEVEN

DEATH SENTENCE

FOR A MOMENT Sarah stared after the stretcher party, as it carried Chad's crushed body away.

'That was no accident,' she said angrily. 'It was a set-up. You murdered Chad!'

Some of the colonists overheard Sarah's words.

'You hear that?' someone shouted. 'They murdered Chad! What's going on here?'

There was a confused murmur of protest.

Commander Ryan raised his voice. 'Quiet, all of you! You all saw what happened. The man Chad opened fire on us. He was a saboteur, a spy. He wanted to ruin the Mars colony – and lose you your jobs!'

White-faced and shocked, the instructor was climbing down from the controls of the giant mining machine.

'There was nothing I could do,' he babbled. 'He fell right under the tracks.'

Commander Ryan ignored his protests. 'Carry on with the instruction session,' he ordered. 'Keep these people busy or there'll be a riot.'

He turned to Sarah. 'As for you – I assure you, if I wanted someone killed I'd arrange it more efficiently than that. The man's death was a lucky accident, that's all. It saved me the trouble of having him shot.' He beckoned to the guards. 'Take these two inside and lock them up. I'll decide what to do with them later.'

The guards marched Tom and Sarah away.

This time they found themselves in a cell and not a guest suite. There were two hard bunks, a toilet compartment, and that was all.

They sat on the bunks, staring gloomily into space.

Sarah was shaken and angry. 'I still think Chad was murdered,' she said.

Tom shook his head. 'I honestly don't think so. Not that Ryan isn't capable of it, mind you. But Chad really did open fire first, you know. And he was shooting at us!'

'But why?' asked Sarah. 'Why would he do that?'

'When he saw us turn up with Ryan and the guards, he must have thought we'd turned him in. He panicked and started shooting and . . . well, you saw what happened.'

Sarah nodded. 'Maybe you're right. Poor Chad . . .'

'I'm sorry about Chad,' said Tom. 'But to be honest, I'm a lot more worried about us. I think we're in real trouble this time.'

'Because of Chad's death?'

'No, because of one of my stupid jokes. You remember that crack I made about *The Revenge of the Martians*?'

'Vaguely. Why's it so important?'

'I went on and said maybe a guard had killed a Martian and the other Martians were taking their revenge. I was just playing with wild ideas, thinking aloud – but did you see how Ryan reacted?'

Sarah said, 'What exactly are you saying, Tom?'

Tom drew a deep breath. 'I think I have stumbled on the truth. I think that's exactly what happened. It's Ryan's most deadly secret. A secret that could get the project closed down and IMC thrown off Mars. And now Ryan thinks we know . . . '

Tom and Sarah passed a long and boring afternoon.

They tried quizzes and word-games to pass the time. But they soon got bored and stretched out on the bunks, trying to relax. It wasn't easy.

At long last a guard appeared. They glimpsed another guard in the corridor behind him. There was no chance of escape.

'What's happening?' demanded Sarah. 'Why have we been locked up? I demand to see the Administrator or Commander Ryan.'

The guard ignored her question. 'I've been told to bring you a meal,' he said.

'About time too,' said Sarah.

The guard ignored this too. 'Come on, then. What do you want?'

'What's going?' asked Tom. 'Is there a menu?'

'You can have anything you like.'

Sarah looked surprised. 'Anything at all?'

'That's right. Anything.'

'Oh dear,' said Tom.

Sarah ordered a large green salad.

Tom ordered steak and chips.

The guard went away.

Before very long, he returned with two trays.

The food was surprisingly good, much better than that served in the dining hall.

Sarah tucked into her salad with enjoyment. 'Do you realise we missed lunch?' she said. 'I'm starving!'

Tom picked at his food in gloomy silence.

'What's wrong?' asked Sarah. 'Don't you like your steak? Have some salad, maybe I can convert you into a veggie!'

'The steak's fine,' said Tom. 'It's real food, I think, probably frozen and shipped out from Earth.'

'Salad's good too,' said Sarah. 'Maybe they grow fresh vegetables here. They could use hydroponics.'

'Hydro-what?'

'It's a way to grow vegetables without soil, you use water and nutrients.' Sarah finished her salad. 'I bet this is what Commander Ryan and the Administrator eat.'

'Very likely.'

'Well, at least they're treating us like VIPs,' said Sarah. 'It's a good sign, don't you think?'

'I'm not so sure.'

'What's the matter with you, Tom?' asked Sarah. 'You've gone all gloomy since they brought us the food.'

'I went all gloomy when the guard said we could have whatever we liked.'

'Why?'

Tom didn't reply.

'Tom!'

Reluctantly Tom said, 'In the bad old days, back on Earth, when they still used to execute people, there was a custom . . .'

'What custom?'

'The condemned man was given a last meal, on the night before the execution.'

'Well, what about it?'

Tom said, 'He could order anything he liked.'

'There's no alternative,' said Commander Ryan. 'They know too much and now they've gone too far. Something the girl said stirred up the colonists, there was nearly a mutiny.'

'We can't afford that sort of thing,' said the Administrator. 'Not at a time like this.'

They were conferring in the Administrator's office.

Commander Ryan sighed. 'There's worse to come,' he said. 'Far worse.'

'Go on.'

'The boy said something about *The Revenge of the Martians*. He said maybe one of my security guards had killed a Martian and the others were after revenge.'

The Administrator jumped up, her face white. *'How does he know? How did he find out?'*

'Muldoon gave him a kind of hint. I think Muldoon knows as well. Or at least suspects.'

'Then arrest him too.'

'I tried. Unfortunately he seems to have disappeared.'

'Then find him!'

'We will. But it will take time. He was here when this base was built, remember. He knows every back tunnel and bolt-hole.'

Slowly the Administrator sat down. 'How could the boy possibly *know*?' she asked again.

'I'm not sure he does know for sure,' said Commander Ryan. 'It may just have been a lucky guess. Or rather, in his case, an unlucky guess. But we can't take the chance.'

'I told you they were dangerous. You're dealing with it?'

'Oh, I'm dealing with it,' said Commander Ryan grimly. 'I can't say I'm happy about it, especially since they're so young. Besides, I rather like them.'

'Will you hold a show-trial? That might quieten the colonists.'

Commander Ryan shook his head. 'I don't think so. It would take too long to arrange, and I want to get this over with. Besides, there really isn't enough evidence for a trial, even for me! We still don't know who sent them or what they're after.'

'We know they're a danger to us,' said the Administrator firmly. 'That's more than enough. How will you arrange it? Another accident?'

'That would look a little suspicious, don't you think? After what's just happened to Chad.'

'What then?'

'The usual,' said Commander Ryan. 'The tried and tested methods are often the best.'

'I see. When?'

'Oh, tonight, I think. These things work better after dark . . .'

The guard opened the door.

'This way.'

They were marched along the corridors to Commander Ryan's office.

He rose to greet them as they came in.

'Ah, there you are! Did you enjoy your supper?'

'Not as much as I might have done,' said Tom grimly.

'I'm sorry to hear that. Why was that?'

'Well, if the occasion was what I think it was . . .'

'I see.' Commander Ryan rubbed his chin. 'I'm sorry if I caused you any distress. I'm a traditionalist, you see. Under the circumstances, I thought it was the least I could do.' He paused, not looking them in the eyes, then turned abruptly. 'Shall we go?' he said. 'No point in putting things off, is there?'

'What are you planning?' asked Sarah. 'Where are we going?'

Commander Ryan still didn't look at her. 'Not far,' he said.

They were marched along more corridors, all silent and deserted. Tom realised it must be late at night.

Well, it would be, he thought.

They ended up at the entrance to the compound where Chad had died. The door was open, and the compound was in semi-darkness. Close by, they could see the huge bulk of the strip-mining machine.

'Well, goodbye,' said Commander Ryan. 'I can't tell you how much I regret this.'

'Not as much as I do,' said Tom grimly. 'What happens now?'

Commander Ryan waved towards the compound. 'All you have to do is walk out of that door. Or run, if you prefer. It won't make any difference.'

'Shot while trying to escape?'

'I told you, I'm a traditionalist,' said Commander Ryan

simply. 'Don't worry, it will be over very quickly. My men are in place and they're all excellent shots.'

Sarah looked from Tom to Commander Ryan.

Tom's foreboding had been all too correct.

They were both going to die . . .

CHAPTER EIGHT

FLIGHT

'WHAT HAPPENS if we refuse to go through the door?' asked Tom.

Commander Ryan tapped the pistol at his belt. 'I should be forced to – take care of things myself. I hope you won't force me to do that. I should find it very painful.'

'You're too sensitive for this job,' said Tom grimly. 'Can we have a few moments alone, to say goodbye?'

'Of course.'

Commander Ryan and the guards stepped back, and Tom led Sarah closer to the open door.

'When I say go, make a dash for it,' he whispered. 'You break left and I'll break right. Run as fast as you can and zigzag. It's pretty dark out there and there's always a chance.'

There's no chance at all, thought Sarah. But there's no point in admitting it!

She leaned forward and kissed Tom on the cheek. 'Right,' she whispered. 'Never say die!'

'OK,' whispered Tom. 'Ready, steady . . .'

There was a sudden roar of engines and the giant strip-mining machine lurched into life. It headed straight towards them, moving surprisingly fast.

'Look out!' shouted Sarah.

'Come on!' yelled Tom. 'Now's our chance!'

They ran out into the compound and dodged around to one side.

The machine roared past them. Far too big for the doorway, it smashed its way through the framework and into the dome.

Running across the compound, Tom and Sarah saw another shape ahead of them. It was a vehicle of some kind, squat and chunky, with huge balloon tires.

A door opened and a hoarse voice called, 'Get in!'

For a moment they hesitated.

From somewhere behind them there came the flash of a gun-muzzle and a bullet zinged off the vehicle. More shots followed.

'Quickly,' urged the voice.

Sarah jumped up into the strange vehicle and Tom followed.

With a grinding of gears the vehicle lurched away, rapidly gathering speed. Its headlights came on, revealing a high barred gate on the far side of the compound.

The chunky vehicle kept moving. It smashed through the gate and disappeared into the darkness beyond . . .

As they bounced across the Martian desert, Tom and Sarah struggled to get their bearings.

They were on the long front seat of a big, square-shaped vehicle. The space behind them was loaded with plastic bottles, crates and containers. To their right, a white-bearded figure crouched over the huge steering wheel.

'Professor Muldoon!' gasped Sarah.

A triumphant cackle came from the driver. 'That's right, young lady. Hold tight, we've got a long way to go.'

'Anything you say, professor,' said Tom. 'A few minutes ago, I didn't think we were going to get anywhere at all.'

Sarah was bursting with curiosity. 'How did you turn up in the nick of time to rescue us? What's this – thing we're riding in? Where are we going?'

'One question at a time, please,' said Professor Muldoon. 'I saw you get arrested, and a contact in security told me what they were planning to do to you. He wasn't too happy about it. Even an IMC security man can have a conscience. He said he drew the line at murdering kids.'

Sarah went on with her questions. 'How did you get that mining-machine thing to crash into the base?'

'Set it going, wedged the controls and jumped out,'

said Professor Muldoon with another triumphant cackle. 'As the instructor said, it's very simple to operate!'

'And what about our transport?' asked Tom. Old vehicles were one of his special interests.

'You're riding in Bessy,' said Professor Muldoon proudly.

'Bessy?'

'A vintage Mars buggy, as used by the early explorers – including me!'

'How did you get hold of it?'

'They kept Bessy on the base here, as a kind of museum piece. Nobody else was interested, so I took her over. I've been maintaining her, keeping the fuel-cells topped up, loading up with supplies. Been driving her all over the Martian desert for years, getting the feel of the planet.'

'Won't the base security people follow us?' asked Tom.

'Can't,' said the professor. 'This is the only piece of old-fashioned working transport on the base. They rely on transmat, you see, between the base and the sub-bases as well as between Mars and Earth. Now transmat isn't working because of the power-leaks, so they're stuck.'

'And where are we going?' asked Sarah.

'We're making for sub-base three.'

'Why sub-base three?'

'I've got good friends there.'

'Last question, professor,' said Tom. 'Why? Why did

you go to all this trouble and risk to help us?'

'Because you talked to me, when you first arrived. You listened, and you didn't laugh.' Muldoon paused. 'And there's another reason.'

'What's that?'

'If I'm going to save the Mars Project I need help.'

'Anything, professor,' said Sarah. 'Anything at all.'

'That's right,' said Tom. 'We owe you our lives. What do you want us to do?'

'For a start, we're going to meet a Martian.'

Sarah gave him a wondering look. 'You're joking, professor! There aren't any Martians.'

'Aren't there?' replied Professor Muldoon mysteriously. 'You wait and see.'

The strip-mining machine smashed its way right to the centre of the main dome before an enterprising guard managed to jump up into its cab and turn it off.

The damage was immense. The air-conditioning was wrecked and there was a partial power failure. It took long hours of work by guards, technicians, bureaucrats and colonists before the base was anything like operational again.

It was late into the night before the Administrator and Commander Ryan could meet in her office for a conference.

'It was Muldoon,' said Commander Ryan bitterly. 'All Muldoon. I'm pretty sure he set the strip-mining machine going. Now that antique Mars buggy of his has disappeared, and he's gone with it.'

'Why?' asked the Administrator explosively. 'What's he up to?'

'Who knows? We should have shipped the old fool back to Earth years ago.'

'Well, we didn't,' said the Administrator. 'And now we can't.'

'And we can't chase after him, either,' said Ryan. 'Not till transmat is fixed, anyway. Any news on that?'

Wearily the Administrator shook her head. 'According to my technicians, there's nothing wrong with the apparatus itself. But try to use it, the power supply drains away. They're still working on it.'

'They'd better hurry,' said Commander Ryan gloomily. 'We can't stall Earth Government much longer – or my corporation, either. No agricultural colony, no mining . . . Much more of this and they'll close us down.'

'And on top of everything else those wretched, trouble-making youngsters escaped.'

'Yes, so they did,' said Commander Ryan. 'To be honest, despite the trouble they've caused, I'm rather pleased about that.' He paused. 'I'd love to know what they're up to now . . .'

Once they got used to the jolting and bouncing – the springing on the Mars buggy left a lot to be desired – Tom and Sarah quite enjoyed the journey.

Not that there was much to see – just the darkness of the endless Martian desert stretching all around. But the buggy was air-conditioned, and there was a plentiful supply of drinks and snacks in the crates in the back.

When Professor Muldoon got too tired to drive, they stopped for the night, parking the Mars buggy in the shelter of a dune.

Tom offered to take over the driving, but Muldoon wouldn't hear of it.

'You have to *feel* your way across the desert by night,' he said, 'and that takes years of experience. If we end up in a ravine, we'll be done for.'

Muldoon wrapped himself in his cloak and stretched out on the front seat, while Tom and Sarah made themselves nests in the piles of supplies in the back.

They woke up cramped and stiff, got out of the vehicle, and had breakfast in the red Martian dawn.

Sarah looked out at the purple desert stretching all around into a hazy distance. 'It's beautiful,' she said.

'I've loved it all my life,' said Professor Muldoon. 'But I'm still not sure it's a place for humans.'

'Who is it meant for, then?' asked Tom.

'Martians, of course,' said Sarah. 'Didn't you say we were going to meet one, professor?'

'I thought you didn't believe in them?' teased Tom.

Sarah smiled. 'After all that's happened to us, I'm ready to believe in anything!'

'Seeing is believing,' said Professor Muldoon solemnly. He raised his hand and pointed.

An incredibly tall, thin figure stood watching them from the crest of a nearby dune.

It was like nothing either Tom or Sarah had ever seen before – and it definitely wasn't human.

'There you are,' said Professor Muldoon. 'Your first Martian . . .'

CHAPTER NINE

MEETING WITH A MARTIAN

THE MARTIAN stood motionless.

They could see it plainly in the clear morning air.

It was man-shaped and immensely tall, a good three metres at least. It had long, thin, spindly arms and legs, a massive torso and a long narrow skull, surmounted by a kind of crest. It stared intently at them with huge green eyes.

The skin was a mottled green, with a scaly look, not unlike that of a lizard.

'It's beautiful,' whispered Sarah. 'Isn't it, Tom?'

If you can call a giant lizard-man beautiful, thought Tom. He nodded, not wanting to spoil Sarah's pleasure.

'It doesn't frighten you or repel you?' asked Professor Muldoon quietly.

Sarah shook her head. 'It looks as if it belongs here.'

'So it does,' said the professor enthusiastically. 'It's perfectly adapted for life on a low-gravity, oxygen-poor desert planet! Look at those legs, those feet. It has huge lungs to get the maximum amount of oxygen from the air.'

'It's certainly very impressive,' said Tom softly.

Professor Muldoon beamed with pleasure at their enthusiasm. 'Let's see if we can get a little closer.'

'If you say so, professor,' said Tom.

Professor Muldoon took a position between Tom and Sarah, a hand on each of their shoulders.

'Move towards it, very slowly. I want it to see you with me, to know you're my friends.'

Slowly and carefully, they walked forward.

When they reached the foot of the dune they stopped, looking up at the tall figure outlined against the sky.

Sarah stared up at it as if hypnotised. It seemed to be staring intently, not at the others but at *her*. She had the strangest feeling that it was trying to tell her something.

After a moment the Martian raised a hand in a kind of farewell salute. It turned and strode gracefully away, disappearing down the other side of the dune.

'Good!' said Professor Muldoon. 'I think it liked you both. Especially you, Sarah!'

'How could you tell?'

'I'm not sure. You're never very sure with Martians. I just sort of felt something.'

'Yes, I know,' said Sarah. 'I felt something too.'

They went back to the Mars buggy and finished breakfast.

'Tell us about the Martians, professor,' urged Sarah.

'I'll try. What is it you want to know?'

'Everything! When did you first see them? Why does nobody else seem to know about them?'

'Are they intelligent?' asked Tom. 'Are there very many of them? Are they friendly?'

Professor Muldoon held up his hand. 'Give me a chance to get a word in and I'll tell you what I can. We'd better get moving again. We can talk on the way.'

They got back into the Mars buggy and resumed their journey.

'The Martians, professor,' urged Sarah, as they bounced and jolted across the desert.

'Yes, come on,' said Tom. 'However did you manage to make friends with them?'

Professor Muldoon said, 'When we humans first came here, before the bases were set up, nobody believed there *were* any Martians. Everyone knew Mars had been a dead planet for millions of years. Things stayed that way at first. But soon after the central base and the first sub-stations were set up, there were occasional sightings, very rare and always from a distance.'

'Didn't it cause a huge fuss?' asked Sarah. 'A discovery like that . . .'

'Not really,' said Professor Muldoon. 'People who said they'd seen a Martian just weren't believed. And once the bases were set up, people only travelled between them by transmat. The Martians seldom went near the bases or the mining areas. And nobody was roaming across the desert any more.'

'Except you?' suggested Tom.

'That's right. Except me. I think the Martians must have got used to me, and realised I was no threat. I tried to make friends, to communicate, but they've always kept their distance. Today's about the closest I've ever been.'

'I'm sure the one we saw was trying to communicate,' said Sarah. 'I had the strangest feeling in my mind. As if it wanted to tell me something . . . Did you feel anything, Tom?'

Tom shook his head. 'Maybe I'm not sensitive enough.'

'I know what you mean, Sarah,' said Professor Muldoon. 'I've felt a sort of twinge of something similar myself occasionally. A sort of message. But I've never been able to make any sense of it. I suppose I'm not sensitive enough either.'

'So you're the only one who knows the Martians exist,' said Sarah.

'I'm afraid not,' said Professor Muldoon sadly. 'Commander Ryan and at least some of his security people know. Not long ago, one of the Martians ventured near the main base. A guard who saw it panicked – and shot it dead.'

'They must believe in the Martians by now, then,' said Tom. 'With the dead body of a Martian for evidence . . .'

'They may believe, but they don't want anyone else to know,' said Professor Muldoon. 'They destroyed the body, hushed up the whole thing.'

Tom looked at Sarah. 'You see? I was right. It was my remarks about *The Revenge of the Martians* that made Ryan finally decide to kill us. I think he was putting it off before. Maybe he's got a soft spot for us. But once we knew the ghastly secret, we had to go!'

'I'm sure you're right,' said Professor Muldoon. 'And it's partly my fault for dropping those stupid hints in front of Commander Ryan. That's another reason why I felt I had to rescue you – I'd done so much to get you into trouble.'

'And the secret's really so important that he had to murder us?' asked Sarah.

Professor Muldoon nodded vigorously. 'The International Mining Corporation has invested huge sums of money in the Mars Project. And if there's any kind of Martian civilisation still in existence then the planet isn't ours – it's theirs. Earth Government would probably insist that the entire Mars Project be closed down.'

'Why haven't *you* sent a message to Earth

Government, professor, telling them what happened?'

'No proof! Ryan destroyed the bodies of both the dead Martian and its killer. The security guard who told me about it is too terrified of Ryan to testify.'

'Surely IMC can't hope to keep the existence of the Martians secret for ever?' said Sarah.

'They're determined to try. They sent out armed patrols with orders to shoot down any Martians they saw.'

Sarah was shocked. 'That's terrible. What happened?'

Professor Muldoon replied, 'Fortunately they didn't see any! Then the power-leaks started and they had other things to worry about.'

'These leaks,' said Tom. 'When did they start?'

'Not long after the Martian was killed.'

'So it looks as if the two things might be connected. The leaks are a kind of Martian counter-attack.'

'Possibly. There were minor power-leaks from the very early days. But recently they've become massive. Transmat uses colossal amounts of energy, you know. Recently, as soon as power builds up it fades away, just vanishes. They can't transmat from Mars to Earth, can't even transmat between the bases any more. And without power the whole terraforming process could go into reverse. The bases would have no food, no air . . .'

'No wonder you said we were doomed,' said Tom.

'I thought if I spread enough alarm and despondency the truth would come out and they'd *have* to do something,' said Professor Muldoon. 'But you saw what happened. They ignored me, told everyone I was mad.'

'But you are going to do something, all the same?' asked Sarah.

'I'm certainly going to try. That's why we're heading for sub-base three. The two scientists running it are good friends of mine. A husband and wife team . . . We're trying to make contact with the Martians. Maybe we can cooperate with them, reach some kind of accommodation. At the very least, we'll try to persuade them to let us use enough power to send everybody home.'

'Are you having any luck?' asked Tom.

'Not so far. But we've got to keep trying. If we don't succeed, every human being on Mars is going to die . . .'

The Administrator stood in Central Operations, impatiently watching the busy technicians all around her.

Commander Ryan strode into the room and came across to her. 'Any progress?'

She shook her head. 'They've checked all the equipment, now they're checking it all again. The transmat apparatus is in order, the generators are working perfectly. We'll build up enough power to try another transmission soon.'

'And lose it all as soon as we start transmission,' said Ryan bitterly. 'And we know who's responsible. Damned scaly green monstrosities.'

The Administrator shot him a warning glance. Officially, the Martians didn't exist. 'Any news of Muldoon and the two spies?' she asked.

'Not exactly news – but I have a theory.'

'Well?'

'One of my security people tells me old Muldoon was always visiting sub-base three. He was very thick with the couple who run it. I bet that's where they're making for.'

'What if they are?' said the Administrator. 'Transmat's down and Muldoon has the only working Mars buggy. There's no way you can go after them.'

'Maybe we can cannibalise enough spares to make a working buggy,' said Ryan thoughtfully. 'I'll check the store rooms. Come to that, I could even take a foot patrol out. It would take a few days, but it might still be worth it.'

'For one old loony and two teenage spies?'

Commander Ryan moved closer and lowered his voice. 'That old loony knows the desert better than anyone on Mars,' he said. 'I'm pretty sure he's in touch with the Martians. At the very least he may know where they are. Find him and we might find them as well. If we destroy their base, we might get the use of our power back.'

'That's a lot of "mights",' said the Administrator mockingly.

Ryan ignored her, following his own train of thought. 'And another thing – *why* did Muldoon go to so much trouble to save those two youngsters and take them with him? There must be a connection, something we don't know about.' Ryan rubbed his chin. He summoned a technician. 'Tell me, what's the name of that married couple, the ones who run sub-base three?'

'Here we are,' said Professor Muldoon. 'Sub-base three.'

It was several hours after their encounter with the Martian. They seemed to have been jolting across the desert for ever. Now, just ahead of them, they saw a small dome, set in a hollow amongst the dunes.

Professor Muldoon drove the Mars buggy to the entrance and they all climbed out.

A slender, dark-haired woman in the usual Mars colony coveralls came to the entrance, waving in welcome.

'There's Helena,' said Professor Muldoon. 'Splendid woman, you'll like her.'

Tom and Sarah looked at each other in consternation.

'Yes,' said Sarah. 'I'm sure we will. Won't we, Tom?'

'Absolutely,' said Tom faintly. 'As a matter of fact, I feel I know her already.'

The woman waving from the doorway was someone they both knew very well. She looked strange in her space coveralls, and she looked tired and anxious as well.

But she was still the woman who'd brought them both up.

She was Tom's mother.

CHAPTER TEN

REUNION

'TOM, SARAH,' said Professor Muldoon. 'This is my friend, Doctor Helena Martin. Helena . . .'

Helena Martin rushed up to Tom and Sarah and hugged them.

'It appears you three already know one another!' said Professor Muldoon in mild surprise.

If he was surprised, Helena Martin was absolutely astounded.

'Tom! Sarah!' she exclaimed. 'This is incredible! What are you doing on Mars? However did you get right out here to sub-base three?'

Tom and Sarah looked at each other. It was a tricky situation to say the least. In every single alternative universe there existed alternative versions of Sarah and Tom and his parents, living their parallel lives. This was the alternative world version of Tom's mother and Sarah's aunt.

Somewhere – back on the Earth in this universe by the sound of it – there were the alternative versions of Tom and Sarah.

Tom had met his alternative parents twice before in different universes, but it was still an unnerving experience.

'It's a long story,' he said, looking desperately to Sarah for help.

'We were worried about you,' said Sarah, thinking fast. 'There were lots of rumours about something going wrong with the Mars Project, so we smuggled ourselves here with the latest batch of colonists.'

'That's right,' said Tom, taking up the story. 'But the security people at the base decided we were spies for some reason. And then we made matters worse by stumbling across some IMC dirty work, and Commander Ryan decided to knock us off!'

Helena Martin looked horrified. 'Kill you, you mean? He actually tried to have you killed? I can't believe it.'

'Believe it!' said Sarah.

'Luckily Professor Muldoon helped us to get away,' concluded Tom. 'He very kindly brought us out here to see you.'

'I didn't know I'd be bringing about a family reunion,' said Professor Muldoon. 'Why didn't you say your parents were here on Mars? Did you say your name was Martin? Yes, I remember now, you did – but I just didn't make the connection.'

'We weren't absolutely sure this was the right base,' said Sarah. 'We didn't want to say anything until we were sure Tom's mother was here.'

'You're both mad,' said Helena Martin. 'Absolutely mad! I don't know what your father will say . . . ' She broke off. 'Not that he's here to say anything at the moment.'

Professor Muldoon looked surprised. 'Peter's not here? Where on Earth – or Mars, rather – has he got to?'

'I wish I knew. He seems to have disappeared. Come inside and I'll tell you all about it.'

Inside the dome they found one large central chamber. It was packed with complicated-looking scientific equipment, and seemed to be a combination living-room and laboratory.

Helena opened and heated food packages, and served them a simple meal.

'So what about Peter?' asked Professor Muldoon as they were eating. 'How long has he been gone?'

'Only a couple of days, but I'm starting to worry.'

'Where has he gone?' asked Tom.

'You know about these mysterious power-leaks?'

Tom nodded.

Helena said, 'Well, you know what a fiend your father is for scientific gadgets?'

Tom glanced quickly at Sarah, who was smiling faintly.

In *their* universe, changing a light bulb was terrifyingly hi-tech as far as Tom's father was concerned. Things were obviously different here.

'Anyway,' Helena continued, 'he was fiddling about for ages, building some kind of tracker gadget. He reckoned he could use it to find out where the leaking power was leaking *to*, if you see what I mean. He asked me to wait till he'd been gone for a few hours, and then to send out two power surges, with a gap in between.'

'So what happened?'

'I sent out the two surges – and in each case the power leaked mysteriously away again.'

'If he could get two trace-readings some distance apart,' said Professor Muldoon, 'he could get a cross-bearing and pinpoint the source of the leaks. In theory, anyway. What a splendid idea! Why didn't I think of that?'

'I wish Peter *hadn't* thought of it,' said Helena. 'If your theories are correct, the most likely source of the power-leaks is the Martian base. They may not appreciate some stray scientist wandering in.'

'I don't think the Martians are necessarily hostile,' said Professor Muldoon. 'Even the power-leaks may just be an attempt to drive us away by relatively peaceful means. All the same . . .'

'All the same, I wish Peter was back here,' said Helena.

'Don't worry, Mum,' said Tom. 'We'll go and find him for you! Won't we, Sarah?'

'Of course, if we can,' said Sarah. 'But how will we know where to look? Unless we build our own tracking device and repeat the experiment.'

'That won't be necessary,' said Professor Muldoon. 'I'm the only tracking device you'll need.'

Tom looked at him in surprise. 'You can track the power-leaks?'

'No, but I can track your father. The Martian desert hasn't been disturbed for millions of years – except by Martians, perhaps. Any human passing over it leaves traces of some kind – traces quite plain to the experienced eye.'

'Splendid!' said Tom, jumping up. 'Let's get started.'

Professor Muldoon didn't move.

'Even the experienced eye requires light, my boy,' he said. 'And soon it will be dark. We'll start first thing in the morning.'

'Well, that's a relief,' said Helena. 'I'll have to stay here, I'm afraid – someone's got to look after the base. But I'm sure you'll find him.' She turned to Sarah. 'Now, you must give me all the news from home. How are the family?'

This time it was Sarah who turned to Tom for help.

'Can we leave the Spanish Inquisition till later, Mum?' he said. 'We've had a long hard day, and if we're starting out first thing tomorrow . . .'

Sarah yawned elaborately. 'I'm very tired, too,' she said. 'I'd really like to turn in.'

Their diversionary tactic worked.

'You must both be exhausted,' said Tom's mother. 'I'll break out some spare sleeping-bags.'

As he drifted off to sleep, Tom heard his alternative world mother and Professor Muldoon talking in low, anxious voices.

He wondered how his alternative world father was getting on with the Martians . . .

They started next morning at dawn – and Tom got to drive the Mars buggy, with Sarah sitting beside him.

Professor Muldoon walked ahead on foot.

As he pointed out, you had to be close to the ground for tracking. It couldn't be done from a moving vehicle.

They followed the tracks, invisible to Tom and Sarah, but apparently quite clear to Muldoon, across the desert.

Progress was slow. They couldn't move any faster than Professor Muldoon could walk. Every now and again he had to come back inside the Mars buggy for rest and refreshment.

The journey took most of a very long day, and dusk was falling when Professor Muldoon came to a sudden halt before a dune. Much larger than the others nearby, it formed a sort of conical hill at the centre of a small hollow.

For a long moment the professor just stood there, staring intently at the ground.

Tom stopped the buggy, and he and Sarah jumped down.

'Have you lost the trail?' called Tom.

'Certainly not!'

'Is it getting too dark to see?' asked Sarah.

'Not yet.'

'What's the problem, then?'

Professor Muldoon beckoned them towards him. 'The problem is this,' he said. 'Your father's tracks lead straight into this dune – and there they stop!'

'You're quite sure?'

'Positive.'

Tom looked at the dune. 'Which presumably means that he's somewhere inside. We'll have to dig him out.'

He shuddered a little. It wasn't pleasant to think of digging the dried-up body of your father – even an alternative world father – out of a hill of Martian sand.

'I'm afraid that's not possible,' said Professor Muldoon. 'Not without digging equipment, anyway. Look at the size of that dune. We could mark it, I suppose, and come back . . .'

'Aren't you both being a bit pessimistic?' asked Sarah.

Tom gave her a puzzled look. 'What do you mean?'

'Well, he couldn't have just walked straight into that dune, could he? It isn't possible. And if the dune had fallen on him somehow I doubt if those tracks would end there so neatly.'

'So what do you think happened?'

'Remember what he was looking for,' said Sarah. 'The

Martian base. Perhaps he found it. Perhaps the entrance is here – inside that dune!'

'Which brings us back to digging,' said Tom despairingly.

'Not necessarily,' replied Sarah softly. Tom saw that she was staring up at the dune with a rapt, almost hypnotised expression on her face.

'Listen!' she said suddenly. 'Did you hear . . . ? I thought I heard something . . .' Her voice trailed away.

Tom listened intently, but the Martian desert was eerily silent as usual.

'What is it, Sarah? I can't hear anything at all.' He turned to Muldoon. 'Can you hear anything, professor?'

Professor Muldoon shook his head. 'No,' he said softly. 'I can't. But you and I, Tom, may not have the right equipment!'

'What do you mean?'

'I don't think she is hearing in quite the usual way, young man. I think she is hearing with her mind.'

'I don't understand.'

'I believe that your cousin Sarah has some sort of rapport with the Martians.'

'A what?'

'Some kind of mental link, a sort of receptivity. I noticed signs of it earlier – when she saw a Martian for the first time. Perhaps it's just a matter of being on the right mental wavelength.'

Tom stared at him unbelievingly. 'Are you serious?'

'Oh yes. I have it myself, though only to a very limited extent. I can sense feelings of curiosity and friendliness, and presumably the Martians sense the same in me. I think Sarah may have the same ability in a much stronger form.'

Tom turned to look at Sarah. She was still staring at the dune in fascination, her head tilted a little, as if hearing distant voices.

Suddenly she raised her arm and pointed. 'Look!'

Sand was sliding down the sides of the dune.

They stepped back in alarm, but the sand showed no signs of piling up around them. Somehow it was absorbed in the surrounding desert.

As more and more of the sand melted away a shape was revealed. Astonishingly, it was a very familiar one.

It was a pyramid!

CHAPTER ELEVEN

INSIDE THE PYRAMID

A PYRAMID – on Mars!

Old legends from Earth flashed through Tom's mind. Didn't some people actually believe that alien visitors from space had taught the Egyptians how to build their pyramids, many thousands of years ago?

Maybe the Martians had visited Earth long before humans had come to Mars. It was an astonishing thought.

Sarah stood gazing at the pyramid, as if waiting for something. 'They're here,' she said with absolute certainty. 'The Martians are here. I can feel it!'

'You realise we're seeing only the very tip of the pyramid,' said Professor Muldoon. 'It's quite clear from its lines that the bulk of it is underground.'

Tom tried to grasp the idea. 'It must be colossal – enormous!'

Professor Muldoon looked around the surrounding

desert. 'And there could be more pyramids, hundreds of them, under all these dunes. One day the desert sands may recede and we shall see the pyramids of Mars!'

'One's quite enough to be going on with,' said Tom. 'What are we supposed to do now? Maybe we should start looking for some kind of door.'

'Look!' said Professor Muldoon. 'Something's happening!'

Three straight-line cracks were appearing at the base of the pyramid. They ran together to form the outline of a triangle.

The triangle slid silently aside, revealing a doorway.

In the doorway a Martian stood waiting.

The Martian had the basic lizard-man shape of the one they'd seen before – but there were differences.

It was even taller and thinner and its mottled skin was of a greyer shade. Somehow Tom got the impression that it was very old. This Martian had a richly-embroidered cloak hanging from its shoulders, and a jewelled, coronet-like head-dress.

Well, this settles the question of their being intelligent, thought Tom. Any race that wears clothes and builds pyramids . . . Not to mention a nifty line in camouflage!

The Martian stepped to one side, indicating the doorway with a sweeping gesture.

The meaning was obvious. They were to go inside.

Tom and the professor looked at each other a little doubtfully, but Sarah moved forward without hesitation. She walked quickly up to the doorway and disappeared inside.

Tom and the professor followed.

Once through the doorway they found themselves in a small, bare ante-chamber. It was lit by a dim glow that seemed to come from the walls.

The Martian raised its hand and the triangular door closed behind them. It raised its hand again. For a moment nothing happened. Then, suddenly, they had the sensation of swift descent. They staggered a little, clutching at each other for support.

'We're in a lift!' whispered Tom. 'A high-speed Martian lift! Going down!'

The sensation stopped as suddenly as it had begun, and another triangular door opened before them.

The Martian led them through it, into an enormous underground chamber, so vast that its ceiling vanished into darkness.

Shadowy and dimly-lit, the great hall contained bank upon bank of strangely-shaped alien machinery. Here and there, more Martians moved silently amongst the gently-glowing apparatus.

Their Martian guide led them across the floor of the hall to an alcove which held a complicated-looking piece of apparatus.

There was a low stone couch underneath it and what looked like several metallic helmets suspended above.

A prone figure was stretched out on the couch. Not a Martian, this time, but a human. And not just any human.

It was Peter Martin, Tom's father and Sarah's uncle.

He seemed to be asleep.

Beside the end of the couch lay a metal box. The box had a revolving aerial and a set of dials set into the lid, and it was fitted with a carrying-strap.

Tom and Sarah rushed to the couch and knelt beside it.

'Dad!' said Tom.

Once again he had the strange experience of seeing the alternate world incarnation of one of his parents.

Except for the silvery Mars Project coveralls, this version looked pretty much the same as the father he knew in his own universe. His face showed signs of strain, though, and he looked both worried and exhausted.

'Uncle Peter!' cried Sarah. 'Are you all right?'

Peter Martin opened his eyes and looked from one to the other of them. 'Tom . . . Sarah,' he muttered. 'I must be having nightmares.'

'That's not very flattering,' said Sarah.

Peter Martin managed a weak grin. 'I didn't mean . . . I must be dreaming, having more hallucinations. That damned machine . . .'

He struggled to rise. 'It's no use, I tell you!' he shouted.

'I can't take it any more. You're wasting your time, nothing's getting through! Leave me alone, damn you . . .'

Tom gripped his shoulder. 'It's all right, Dad. Don't worry, it isn't a nightmare, or even a dream. We're really here!'

'But it's impossible,' said his father feebly. 'You're both back on Earth. How could you possibly be here? It's that damned machine, it's driven me mad.'

'No it hasn't, Uncle Peter,' said Sarah. 'I promise you, we really are here.'

Peter Martin struggled to calm himself. He squeezed Tom's shoulder. 'You're real! But how did you get here?'

'Here on Mars?' said Tom. 'Well, that's a long story! We're here at the pyramid because we came to find you. What's been happening to you?'

His father struggled into a sitting position. 'I made this tracking scanner . . .' He waved towards the box by the end of the couch.

'Mum told us,' said Tom. 'And it led you here.'

Peter Martin struggled to clarify his thoughts. 'I was amazed when the pyramid appeared. And when they invited me inside . . .'

'What happened then?' asked Sarah.

'They connected me to this machine here. I think it's some kind of communications set-up.'

'Did it work?' asked Professor Muldoon eagerly.

Peter Martin shook his head, and then winced,

clutching at his temples. 'All it did was give me some very nasty hallucinations and a splitting headache. They gave up eventually and let me rest. I must have fallen asleep . . .' He rubbed his forehead. 'Look, what are you two doing here? And you, Muldoon? However did you all find me?'

'Professor Muldoon here followed your tracks,' said Tom. 'I tell you, those Native American trackers in old Western movies have got nothing on him!'

'But how did you two get to Mars? Do I gather you've seen your mother, Tom? Is she all right?'

The Martian stepped forward, cutting off the flow of questions. It pointed to the communications apparatus. Then it pointed to Sarah. The meaning was unmistakable.

Peter Martin jumped up, staggering a little. 'No! You're not putting her in that thing!'

Once again the Martian pointed, first to the communications apparatus, then to Sarah.

'It's all right, Uncle Peter,' said Sarah. 'I want to try.'

'But you don't know what it's like!'

'They won't harm her, Peter,' said Professor Muldoon.

'Not intentionally, perhaps, but . . .'

'It'll be all right,' said Sarah.

'Are you sure you want to do this, Sarah?' asked Tom anxiously. 'Let me have a go.'

Sarah shook her head. 'Someone's got to communicate with the Martians if we're ever going to sort things out here. They seem to think I'm the most likely prospect.'

Sarah took her uncle's place on the couch.

The Martian lowered one of the helmets on to her head, and fitted another on to its own. It adjusted controls and the communications device hummed into life. Immediately Sarah sat up, her face twisted with pain.

Peter Martin stepped forward, but Professor Muldoon restrained him with a hand on his arm.

The Martian's long, claw-like fingers made rapid adjustments to the controls.

Gradually Sarah's face relaxed and she settled back on to the couch. She lay there, eyes wide open, staring into space for what seemed like a very long time.

The Martian stood poised, motionless at the machine. Occasionally it made another minute adjustment to the controls.

Suddenly Sarah sat up, pulling the helmet from her head. 'I don't know, I tell you, I just don't know!'

Tom hurried over to her. 'Are you all right?'

'I'm fine. Just a bit overwhelmed.'

'What happened?' asked Professor Muldoon eagerly. 'What did you experience?'

'We – communicated,' said Sarah. 'Like a voice inside my head.'

'A telepathic amplification device,' muttered Muldoon. 'What was communicated? What was said?'

'The message was that when Uncle Peter arrived with his tracking device, they hoped he might be sufficiently intelligent to communicate with – but he wasn't! Sorry, Uncle Peter. When I turned up they could sense enough even without the machine to know I was the one.'

'You say "they", not "it",' said Professor Muldoon.

Sarah shrugged. 'I know. Somehow I felt I was talking to all of them.'

'If the Martians are telepathic they may share a group consciousness,' said Professor Muldoon. 'What one knows, they all know. Speak to one and you speak to them all.'

'Harm one and you harm them all,' said Tom. 'Remember, a security guard shot one of them. Maybe they all know what happened.'

'Ask if that's why they're draining our power,' said Peter Martin.

Sarah replaced the helmet and lay back for a time. Then she took off the helmet and sat up. She started speaking again in a low, dreamy voice.

'When their planet began to die, millions of years ago, the Martians built these underground bases and put themselves into hibernation. When the humans came to Mars and started terraforming, the energy they pumped into the planet revived some of the Martians.' She looked at Professor Muldoon. 'I don't really understand this bit, but the Martians have some way of gaining direct access to energy sources. Through the ground or through the atmosphere, I don't know ... Anyway, they took just a little energy at first, but when one of them was killed they took all they could get. They're storing it until they have enough to revive all their fellow-Martians.'

'What are they going to do then?' asked Tom.

'They seem to be a bit divided on that,' said Sarah. 'They may share a group consciousness but there seems to be plenty of different opinions. As far as I can make out, there are three different groups, like families or clans, all with different ideas.'

'What are they?' asked Professor Muldoon impatiently. 'What do they want?'

Sarah paused, gathering her – or rather the Martians' – thoughts.

'The first group, led by the one who brought us here, wants to work out some compromise with the humans.'

'And the others?'

'They want to enslave the humans and make them go on producing energy for the Martians.'

'And the last?'

'The last group is the clan of the Martian who was killed by the security guard.'

'And what do they want?'

'To exterminate every human being on Mars.'

CHAPTER TWELVE

CAPTURE

A LITTLE silence followed Sarah's announcement.

'Do you think you can persuade them to go for the first option?' asked Tom.

'I don't think I can persuade them to do anything,' said Sarah. 'I'm just an interpreter. All I can do is give them all the information I can and let them make up their own minds.'

'We must convince them of the value of negotiation,' said Professor Muldoon fiercely. 'It's for their own good just as much as for ours.'

'Yes, but will they see it that way?' asked Tom.

'They most certainly ought to!' said the professor. 'With all our faults, we humans brought Mars – and the Martians – back to life, after all. Without our enterprise and our energy, they'd still be fast asleep! It's IMC that's their enemy, not mankind.'

'I think they might find it rather hard to tell the difference,' said Sarah.

Tom grinned. 'You mean we all look alike to them!'

'Not exactly,' said Sarah. 'But they're puzzled by the fact that some humans are like us, whereas others are like the IMC security guards. The Martians are not like that.'

'How do you mean?'

'I don't think they vary as much as we do. At least, not to such extremes.'

'Exterminating the entire Mars colony sounds pretty extreme to me,' said Tom.

'Yes, but remember how much they were provoked. To kill another living being is a shocking thing to them. I think that's why they've held off from attacking the Mars base for so long.'

'We must explain the more positive side of humanity to them,' said Professor Muldoon. 'We must persuade them to negotiate.'

'The thing is,' said Sarah, 'they've got hundreds and hundreds of questions about humans and about the Mars Project and I can't answer any of them. They need to talk to you, professor.'

'Well, I'd be happy to try.' He gave the communications device a dubious glance. 'If that thing will work on me . . .'

'It doesn't have to,' said Sarah. 'I'll interpret. They can talk to you through me! I'll tell them . . .'

She put the helmet back on and resumed her communication with the silent Martians.

Peter Martin staggered a little, and Tom and Professor Muldoon helped him to sit on the end of the couch.

'We ought to get you back to the sub-base,' said Tom. 'Sarah, ask them if we can go.'

After a moment Sarah said, 'You and your dad can go, Tom. But they're anxious to start talking to Professor Muldoon right away.'

'Well I'm not leaving you here.'

'I'll be fine, Tom, honestly. The professor will be with me, remember.' Sarah thought for a moment. 'Look, you take your dad back to sub-base three, so your mother can look after him. You can use the Mars buggy. When you've got him settled, come back here for us.'

'An excellent scheme,' said Professor Muldoon. 'These discussions are too important to be delayed.'

'How will I find my way back to the base – and then back here afterwards?'

'Follow the buggy tracks both ways. You can't miss them.'

After some more persuasion, Tom agreed. He was worried about his father and it seemed the only thing to do.

They said their goodbyes, and another Martian escorted Tom and his father out of the pyramid and back to the Mars buggy.

The Martian disappeared inside the pyramid, and Tom helped his father to climb into the front seat of the Mars buggy.

He heard the hissing of moving sand, and saw that the sands were rising rapidly up the sides of the pyramid. More and more sand followed, until the pyramid was just a sand dune, like all the others.

'Amazing!' said Tom.

He got behind the steering wheel of the Mars buggy, pulled the starter-lever and drove away.

He glanced quickly at his father and saw that he was already asleep.

It was easy enough for Tom to retrace his route by following the tracks. Since he didn't have to go at a walking pace the journey went much quicker and it wasn't too long before the dome of sub-base three came into sight.

Tom's mother came rushing out as the Mars buggy pulled up by the entrance. Tom shook his father awake and helped him to get out of the buggy.

Helena was torn between anxiety and relief.

'You found him! He looks dreadful, what happened to him? Where are the others?'

'I think Dad's all right really. He's just exhausted, mentally and physically. The others are all right too – at least, I hope they are. Let's get Dad inside and into bed, and I'll tell you all about it.'

* * *

Helena handed Tom a ham sandwich and a steaming beaker of coffee. 'Let me see if I've got this straight,' she said. 'Professor Muldoon put his nose to the ground and tracked your father to a pyramid, buried inside a sand dune and filled with Martians. You all had a nice little chat, and then you drove your dad home, leaving Sarah and Muldoon playing telepathic twenty questions with the Martian high priests?'

Tom grinned affectionately at her as he chomped his ham sandwich. In alternative worlds he'd seen his mother as the plump wife of an SS gauleiter and as a leading transmat scientist. Here she was very much the mother he had always known, capable and decisive and nobody's fool.

'It sounds a bit much when you put it like that – but that's about the strength of it. I only hope Professor Muldoon can work out some kind of deal with the Martians; it's our only hope, really.' He swallowed the last of his sandwich and swigged down his coffee. 'I'd better get back to Sarah and the professor. I feel like I'm running a Martian minicab service!'

'A what?'

'Just something they had back on Earth, before transmat.' Tom stood up. 'I really must get going.'

'And what do I do while you and Sarah go gallivanting about?' snapped his mother, following him to the door. 'Smooth your father's fevered brow and get on with some light dusting?'

Tom grinned. She'd never really been the domestic type. He bent down and gave her a farewell kiss on the cheek. 'Look after Dad, keep the base running, keep your head down and wait until we all come back. With any luck we'll have a better idea of what's going on.'

Waving goodbye, he got behind the wheel of the Mars buggy and drove away.

The tracks were deeper now, and easy enough to follow. Tom wondered how he was going to get back inside the hidden pyramid when he reached it. Maybe the Martians had some kind of scanning system and would see he was there. If not – well, there was plenty of food and water in the back of the buggy. He'd just have to camp out by the dune until they turned up. If they turned up.

Maybe the Martians would opt for the extermination plan – and start with the professor and Sarah. Then they'd all swarm out of the pyramid and start on him!

Telling himself not to be so negative, Tom drove on his way. It was getting dark, he noticed, and with alarming speed. Apparently Mars didn't go in for long twilights.

How am I going to follow the tracks in the dark? he wondered.

'By switching on the headlights!' he answered himself. Presumably the Mars buggy had headlights of some kind.

He was studying the unfamiliar controls when a spotlight from a nearby dune bathed the Mars buggy in a harsh white light.

An amplified voice bellowed, 'Stop the vehicle. You are surrounded! Get out with your hands up!'

'You wish!' yelled Tom. He swung the Mars buggy in a wide turn and headed back the way he had come. Shots spanged off the back of the buggy and, seconds later, he heard the roar of some kind of engine.

Old Ryan must have come up with some transport after all, he thought. It's probably some kind of lash-up, though. Maybe I can out-run them. Come on, Bessy!

Driving dangerously fast, and choosing his route by memory and instinct, Tom sped towards sub-base three. Was the engine sound behind him growing fainter?

He needed to reach the base well ahead of his pursuers, to give him time to get his parents into the buggy and take off again. With any luck he could lose the other vehicle in the desert.

Then what? he thought. I don't want to lead them back to the pyramid. Maybe Dad will know some good hiding-place. Or we could just hide out in the desert till they give up and go away. Plenty of supplies in the buggy!

The lights of sub-base three appeared ahead.

Tom zoomed down into the little hollow and stopped the buggy close to the open front door.

He ran inside, yelling, 'Mum, Dad, don't argue, jump in the buggy!'

His parents were standing side by side in the middle of the little dome. They looked strained and tense, and there was something unnatural in the way they stood, just looking at him, without moving or speaking.

'Don't just stand there, get moving,' he said urgently. 'Commander Ryan is . . .'

A familiar, mocking voice interrupted him. 'Commander Ryan is ahead of you for once.'

Immaculate as ever in his ornate black uniform, Commander Ryan strolled out of the sleeping area.

He was flanked by two IMC security guards, both with guns in their hands.

CHAPTER THIRTEEN

FIRING-SQUAD

COMMANDER RYAN strolled over to Tom and tapped him lightly under the chin with one black-gloved fist.

'You never really got the hang of "Shot while trying to escape", did you?'

'I thought we managed rather well,' said Tom. 'For a couple of beginners, anyway.'

'No, no, no!' said Commander Ryan reprovingly. 'You got it all wrong. You weren't supposed to escape, you know.'

'We weren't?'

'No, you were supposed to get shot!'

'I'll try and do better next time,' said Tom.

'There isn't going to be a next time. Well, not in quite the same way.'

'You've decided I'm innocent?'

'No, I've decided on a show trial, followed by a public

execution by firing-squad. Discipline is getting a bit slack at the base, after your friend Muldoon's escapade and your escape. Our colonists are starting to get above themselves.'

'And you think having me shot will calm them down?'

'A good public execution always helps to restore law and order. Besides, a firing-squad is always so splendidly melodramatic, isn't it? You're not an old movie buff by any chance?'

'As a matter of fact, I am.'

'I knew we had a lot in common. I don't suppose you smoke, do you?'

'No, I don't.'

'What a pity!'

'Why?'

'It's all part of the ritual,' explained Commander Ryan. 'The blindfold, the last cigarette. I told you, I'm a traditionalist. A last ice cream doesn't work nearly so well.'

An idea struck him. 'You wouldn't care to start smoking, would you? It wouldn't be for long.'

'Not really,' said Tom. 'They say it's bad for your health.'

Commander Ryan laughed. 'I'm going to miss you, Tom, I really am. But I assure you, the firing-squad won't!'

Tom's mother was listening to their macabre conversation with unbelieving horror. 'What's all this talk about shooting? Tom may have come to Mars a little irregularly, but that's scarcely a capital offence.'

'Tom is involved in a good deal more than illicit travel,' said Commander Ryan. 'And so, I suspect, are you and your husband.'

He looked at Tom. 'And where are the rest of the conspirators? Your delightful cousin and mad Professor Muldoon?'

Tom had been thinking furiously. He had to come up with some kind of cover story, however feeble. One that contained no reference to Martian pyramids, no mention of the present whereabouts of Sarah and Muldoon.

'I've no idea,' he said.

'Are you going to cooperate or not?' demanded Ryan. 'I assure you, it will make your last few hours considerably more pleasant. Not to mention those of your parents.'

'Certainly, I'll cooperate,' said Tom. 'I'll tell you anything you want to know.'

Ryan gave him a suspicious glare. 'Then you can start with explaining your presence at this sub-base.'

'Isn't it obvious? After all, we only came to Mars to see our parents.'

'Why didn't you tell me you had relatives on Mars?'

'Somehow I didn't think you'd be sympathetic. We weren't even sure how our parents would react, we wanted to sound things out.'

'Go on.'

'When you got your daft idea about our being spies we decided to come out here. When we arrived, Dad had wandered off into the desert and got lost. We went to look for him in the buggy, and separated to search on foot.'

'And what happened to the professor and your cousin? Managed to mislay them, did you?'

'In a way,' said Tom. 'By the time I found Dad, I'd lost track of the others. I was worried about Dad so I brought him back here first. I was going back to look for the others when your lot turned up.' Tom looked hard at his mother. 'That's right, isn't it, Mum?'

'Absolutely right,' said his mother steadily. 'That's exactly what happened.'

'That's right,' said Tom's father. 'I can confirm it in every detail.'

'I don't think I believe you, somehow,' said Commander Ryan. 'But I'll get the truth out of you.' He looked at his three prisoners. 'It will all be so very much easier now. You're going to be much more anxious to be helpful, all of you, positively eager, in fact.'

'Don't bank on it.'

'Oh, but I do! People who can withstand pressure by themselves are much more persuadable when they see it applied to someone they care for. Will you confess everything to save your parents, Tom? Or will they confess to anything to save you? One or the other, I'm sure of that!'

Peter Martin suddenly moved towards Commander Ryan. 'You lousy . . .'

'Leave it, Dad,' said Tom quickly. 'The commander

likes his little joke – and since he's backed by two armed thugs we'd better laugh as well.'

They heard the sound of a vehicle drawing up outside. A security guard rushed in. 'We lost him, sir . . .' He broke off at the sight of Tom.

'Of course you did,' said Commander Ryan. 'Luckily I didn't!' He rubbed his chin thoughtfully. 'I think we'll continue this discussion back at main base. I feel a little isolated here in the desert. You never quite know what's out there.'

You don't know how true that is! thought Tom.

He wondered how Sarah and the professor were getting on in the Martian pyramid.

Ryan nodded to the guards. 'Take the prisoners outside.'

The guards escorted Tom and his parents out of the dome, and Commander Ryan followed.

Parked next to the Mars buggy was a strange-looking vehicle. It was an oddly-shaped flat-bed truck with big tractor wheels.

Crowded into the back, looking very uncomfortable, were half a dozen armed security guards.

Despite the seriousness of his situation, Tom couldn't help laughing. 'Don't think much of yours,' he said.

'Pathetic, isn't it?' said Commander Ryan cheerfully. 'Botched together out of some bits of mining machinery. Still, it got us here, and with any luck it'll get us back.'

He looked thoughtfully at the Mars buggy, and then turned to Tom. 'I'll let you drive me back in this thing, I think. It looks far more comfortable.'

'Martian minicabs at your service,' said Tom.

Commander Ryan drew his pistol. 'You and your parents can go in the front, I'll be in the back with this. Try any tricks and I assure you I'll shoot either your mother or your father.'

Tom helped his parents into the front seat of the Mars buggy and got behind the wheel.

Commander Ryan got in the back and settled himself amongst the supplies. 'Just follow the truck,' he ordered.

The guard truck switched on its lights and drove away. Tom looked for the Mars buggy's headlight switch, and found it this time. He switched on the lights and followed the guard truck out of the hollow.

From the shadows at the edge of the desert, a tall, thin figure stood watching.

Sarah and Professor Muldoon were sitting side by side on the stone couch. It wasn't all that comfortable.

Some distance away in the gloom, the Martian that Sarah had communicated with was standing in a semi-circle with two others, locked in silent communion.

Sarah thought they were probably the leaders of the other two clans, the slavery party and the extermination group. Her main hope was that *their* Martian, as she thought of it, seemed to be the senior. Perhaps it would persuade the two others . . .

Professor Muldoon had talked himself hoarse, urging the benefits of a Martian alliance with mankind, struggling to convince them that all men weren't like Ryan and his guards.

Sarah had transmitted his words through the telepathic amplifier.

Now the Martians were considering his arguments.

'I suppose those three are clan chiefs, or high priests or something,' said Sarah.

'If they even have chiefs and priests,' said Professor Muldoon. 'Perhaps they're all equal. We know so little about them.'

'I don't think much of Martian hospitality,' said Sarah. 'You'd think they'd have offered us a cup of tea by now.'

'We don't even know if they eat or drink! Maybe they live on pure energy. They seem to have some kind of affinity with it.'

'They don't seem to know how to create it any more,' Sarah pointed out. 'Why else do they keep stealing yours?'

'So many unanswered questions,' sighed Professor Muldoon.

One of the Martians, *their* Martian, broke off from the group and came over to them. It went to the amplifier and fitted on one of the helmets.

Hastily, Sarah did the same. Anxiously she 'listened'

to the flow of the Martian's thoughts. Then she turned to the professor and smiled. 'It's all right. They've agreed to give collaboration a try. They want *you* to negotiate for them.'

'Willingly! What wonderful news.'

'Wait, there's something else,' said Sarah. 'Not such good news. A bunch of security guards turned up in some kind of vehicle and took Tom and his parents away. We've got to help them, professor!'

Professor Muldoon jumped up. He looked around the vast shadowy chamber and at the silently waiting Martians – their new allies.

He took Sarah's hands. 'Don't worry, my dear. We will!'

CHAPTER FOURTEEN

ALLIANCE

ONCE AGAIN Tom found himself in one of Commander Ryan's security cells.

This time, instead of Sarah, he had his parents for company. At least, his alternate world parents. The more time he spent with them, the more the distinction blurred. It wasn't surprising, really. They were so exactly like his parents.

They *were* his parents . . .

I wonder if I should tell them I'm not really their son, he thought. At least, not the version they think I am. It might help them to know that the this-world Tom and Sarah are still somewhere back on Earth, presumably safe and sound. On the other hand it would only confuse them – and they'd never believe me.

Tom's mother was still furious about the way they had been treated. 'I shall give Commander Ryan a piece of my mind when I next see him,' she declared. 'Locking us up like this for no reason at all. Threatening to shoot us, indeed! He must be mad.'

'I think he is,' said Tom. 'He's been under a heck of a strain for a very long time. Even in the short time I've known him, I think I've seen him get steadily worse. At least he seemed to have a bit of a conscience about killing us at first. Now he's perfectly prepared to shoot all three of us, just to scare the colonists into submission.'

'But what exactly is Ryan accusing us of?' asked Tom's father.

'I think your main crime is being my parents,' said Tom. 'Sorry about that!'

'And what about you? What are you and Sarah supposed to have done that merits a firing-squad?'

Tom shrugged. 'Espionage, sabotage, treason – you name it. Oh, and being an accessory to the wanton destruction of IMC property!'

'Rubbish!' said his mother. 'Of all the nonsense . . .'

'Well, the last bit's true, to be fair,' said Tom. 'Things did get smashed up a bit when we escaped with Professor Muldoon.'

'Escaped what? And why?' demanded his mother exasperatedly.

Tom gave his parents a potted version of what had happened when he and Sarah had first arrived.

'But what made Commander Ryan decide you were

spies?' demanded his father. 'Just because you ran into this man Chad . . .'

'Who really was a spy . . .' said Tom. 'Guilt by association, you see.'

'But that's absurd,' protested his mother.

Tom made a last attempt to make her understand. 'The thing about Commander Ryan is, he's panicky and he's paranoid. The Mars Project has gone wrong from the start, he can't send back any minerals, he can't even get back to Earth. He's worried about losing his job – losing everything – and so is his mate, that Administrator woman. Now the colonists are giving him trouble. On top of all that, he's got the Martians to worry about. As far as he's concerned, they're the biggest problem of all. They endanger everything he wants, simply by their existence.'

'What do you mean?' asked his father.

'If the secret gets out that there really are Martians, the Mars Project may be cancelled,' said Tom. 'You and I *know* the Martians exist, we've seen them. Sarah's communicated with them. We all know too much. Ryan doesn't dare to risk that whatever information we have uncovered gets to Earth.'

'Even so,' said Tom's father, 'I still can't really believe he'll go through with this firing-squad nonsense.'

'I can,' said Tom grimly. 'It's quite mad – but it's practical, in a way, at least from his point of view.'

'Why?' asked Peter Martin impatiently. 'What possible

good will it do him to shoot three completely innocent people?'

'Quite a lot,' said Tom. 'It provides him with a nice little spy conspiracy, backed up by a few dramatic executions. It gives him someone to blame for all the Mars Project's problems and it buys him some time . . .'

'What about Muldoon and Sarah?' asked Tom's mother. 'Surely they'll . . .'

Tom shook his head hard and put a gentle hand over his mother's mouth. 'Don't say anything you don't want to broadcast, Mum,' he warned her quietly.

His mother nodded her understanding. With a visible effort, she clamped her mouth tightly shut.

For a little while longer they awaited their fate in silence. Then the cell door opened and a couple of guards appeared.

They marched Tom and his parents out of the cell, along now-familiar corridors and into the Administrator's office. Commander Ryan and the Administrator were waiting for them.

'We're all ready for you,' said Commander Ryan.

'One last chance,' said the Administrator. 'Will you tell us where we can find the girl and that old fool Muldoon?'

'Would it make any difference?' asked Tom.

'To be honest, no,' said Ryan. 'We've got the audience all assembled, we can't let them down.' He turned to Tom. 'You're sure about that last cigarette?'

Tom's mother gave Commander Ryan a look of angry disdain. 'May I ask what you propose to do with us?'

'Shoot you, of course,' said Ryan calmly.

Tom's father was furious. 'Without a trial?'

'I've decided not to bother with a show trial,' said Commander Ryan. 'Such a bore, really, especially when one already knows the result. Don't worry, I've taken care of all the necessary paperwork.' Commander Ryan shuffled some papers on his desk. 'Confessions all in order, execution warrants signed.' He stood up. 'This way, please.'

The Administrator and Commander Ryan strode from the room.

The guards closed in behind the prisoners and Tom and his parents followed.

There didn't seem anything else to do.

They were taken to the big compound with the row of transmat booths – the one where Tom and Sarah had first arrived.

It was brightly lit now, and filled with a milling crowd of colonists. They seemed excited and worried at the same time – as if they knew something was going to happen, but weren't too sure they'd enjoy it.

In the centre of the crowd, a squad of guards created a circle of space.

On the far side of the compound, six rifle-carrying guards stood at attention before a section of blank wall.

With a sudden chill, Tom realised that this must be the firing-squad.

His parents looked round in amazement, as if unable to take in what was happening to them.

The little group moved to the open circle, and Commander Ryan raised his voice. 'Your attention, please!' he boomed.

The crowd fell silent, watching him curiously.

Commander Ryan began talking. The deep, compelling voice had a soothing, almost hypnotic quality. 'As you all know, our Mars Project has been plagued with problems,' he said. 'At first we assumed they were inevitable teething troubles – but in fact they were caused by the actions of a group of spies and saboteurs. Their treachery endangered the bright future you all deserve. One of them, the man Chad, died in an accident while resisting arrest. Some of you saw that. Now you will see the execution of three more spies.'

Tom's father shouted, 'Lies! It's all . . .' He broke off with a grunt as a guard's rifle-butt thudded into his back.

'I'll make the speeches, if you don't mind,' said Commander Ryan quietly. 'Besides, you'd be wasting your time. They'd never believe you.'

Tom's mother hugged her husband fiercely, as he clenched his teeth in pain. 'They're going to shoot us,' she whispered. 'They're really going to shoot us.'

Tom patted her on the back. 'Don't give up yet, Mum. Never say die!'

Commander Ryan raised his voice again. 'Two of the conspirators are still at large, but their capture is inevitable. Now it is time for these three to meet the fate they deserve.'

He turned to Tom. 'Would you like to go in any particular order?' he asked politely. 'Or shall I choose for you?'

Before he could reply – and Tom wondered afterwards, with a shudder, how he *would* have replied – another voice rang out.

'Everything Commander Ryan has told you is a lie!'

Everyone in the crowd turned.

Professor Muldoon was standing in the doorway to the dome. Sarah appeared beside him.

Commander Ryan was delighted. 'The rest of the group,' he said. 'Two more items for the programme – five executions!'

Professor Muldoon spoke again. 'The three people you were about to see executed – no, not executed but murdered – by Commander Ryan are innocent. They are not spies or saboteurs. Apart from the unfortunate man Chad, there are no spies or saboteurs. These charges are inventions of Commander Ryan and the Administrator, clumsy attempts to cover up their own incompetence.'

Someone in the crowd shouted, 'If there's no sabotage, what about the power losses?'

'And why won't transmat work any more?' yelled someone else.

'Why can't we even contact Earth?' called another voice.

'I shall tell you,' said Professor Muldoon impressively. 'All these troubles were caused by the actions of the original inhabitants of this planet. The Martians!'

Professor Muldoon and Sarah stepped aside. Between them appeared the tall figure of a Martian.

There were murmurs of fear and astonishment from the crowd.

Commander Ryan's face twisted with rage. 'Damned slimy monsters!'

He drew his pistol, took aim at the impassive Martian – and froze as the pistol flew from his hand, spinning high in the air.

'Telekinesis,' said Professor Muldoon. 'Power of the mind. The Martian you killed was unsuspecting, taken by surprise. This one is not. It could just as easily stop your heart – or the flow of blood to your brain. Your guard may have killed one Martian before, but no more – they will not tolerate your aggression.'

A panic-stricken guard raised his rifle – and collapsed, clutching at his chest.

The crowd gasped with fear.

'There is no need to be afraid,' said Professor Muldoon. 'The Martians are now our allies – our friends.'

The crowd didn't seem too convinced. A panicky voice called, 'How can we be sure?'

'I will prove it to you. All the normal functions of the base are now restored. I have already sent a full account of recent events to Earth Government. Martial law will be imposed and a full enquiry held. A treaty with the Martians will be signed. Our friends from Earth are already on the way. Indeed, they are here!'

Suddenly the row of transmat booths across the back of the compound lit up. People poured out in a continuous stream.

There were armed soldiers in the khaki uniforms and blue berets of the army of Earth. They all seemed to have been well briefed beforehand, and each group of soldiers had its own particular target.

Some quickly moved in on the security guards, disarming them and marching them away.

Two soldiers checked a computerised Identikit photograph and closed in on the indignant Administrator.

'You can't arrest me!' she protested. 'I am the Administrator. I'm in charge here. Besides, Commander Ryan is the man you really want. He's the one responsible for all these crimes. I was simply a pawn, helpless in his hands.'

The soldiers took her away.

More and more people poured out of the transmat booths. There were stern-looking officials, diplomats, even an ambassador in full diplomatic uniform, who bowed low before the astonished Martian.

'On behalf of the people of Earth, greetings. It is my earnest hope that this day marks an era of peace and cooperation between our two species.'

Tom and his parents, meanwhile, were enjoying a joyful reunion with Sarah and Professor Muldoon.

'How'd you like to translate all that, Sarah?' said Tom as the ambassador droned on.

'I think I'd prefer the firing-squad.'

She hugged Tom and his parents. 'I'm so glad you're all right . . .'

'Cut it a bit fine, didn't you?' grumbled Tom, hugging her affectionately in return.

'Well, we had to walk across the desert, for a start,' said Sarah. 'You went off with the Mars buggy!'

'And there was a lot to do when we got here,' said Professor Muldoon. 'We had to take over the control room, with the assistance of our Martian friends. I had to restore power to all the systems, send a full report to Earth . . .'

A voice said, 'If I may interrupt this happy occasion for a moment . . .'

They turned and saw Commander Ryan, flanked by two Earth soldiers.

'I'm off to Earth, so I just thought I'd say goodbye. I'm so glad we didn't have to go through with our little ceremony.'

He paused. 'It looks as if I may be in for rather a

difficult time. I don't suppose you two young people would care to put in a good word for me at my trial?'

'A good word?' said Sarah indignantly. 'You were going to have me shot!'

'You were going to have me shot twice!' said Tom. 'And my parents.'

'Always with the greatest reluctance, I assure you. Ah well, it's been nice knowing you — at least, until now!'

Commander Ryan nodded coolly and strolled away.

'The Administrator is the one you really want,' they heard him telling the fascinated soldiers. 'Dreadful woman! She was in charge, you know. I was just obeying orders . . .'

'Cheek,' said Sarah. 'I bet he talks his way out of it.'

'Not if I have anything to do with it!' said Tom's mother. 'I'll put in a word for him, all right! Nobody tries to shoot my husband and my children and gets away with it!'

Two transmat booths lit up, and two figures emerged. They looked around the compound and then ran eagerly across to the little group.

'Mum, Dad!' said the boy. 'Are you all right?'

The girl said, 'We heard what was going on and made the authorities let us come.'

The two new arrivals were the other Tom and Sarah. The this-world Tom and Sarah. And the two pairs couldn't coexist for long in the same universe.

Tom took Sarah's arm. 'Come on, let's go for it. It's as good a chance as any.'

She stared at him. 'Chance of what?'

'To get home, of course! Or do you want to stick around for the explanations?'

Tom went up to the two newcomers and shook his astonished other self firmly by the hand.

'Nice to see you at last. Glad you could make it!'

Sarah gave her other self a friendly hug.

'Have a lovely time on Mars!'

Then they both disappeared.

CHAPTER FIFTEEN

HOME-COMING

A STRANGE, timeless period of swirling disorientation . . .

Tom had his eyes tightly shut. He opened them, very cautiously.

He was sitting on a bench in Trafalgar Square.

Sarah was sitting beside him, her eyes still shut.

Tom looked around him.

It was a fine, sunny day. Pigeons were fluttering around the square.

Tourists of all sizes, shapes and colours were wandering about. They were wearing everyday casual clothes.

So was he, Tom realised, glancing down at himself.

There were no noisy, smelly cars trundling round the square.

It looked as if transmat was working all right here.

But there was still the ultimate test.

Almost reluctantly, Tom raised his eyes to the figure

on top of the tall column. He gave a huge sigh of relief.

It was Nelson.

Not Hitler, not Napoleon, but Nelson.

Good old Nelson. One arm, one eye, the lot.

He touched Sarah's shoulder. 'It's all right, you can open your eyes. I think we're home.'

Sarah kept her eyes tightly shut. 'You're sure?'

'Pretty sure.'

'No Nazis?'

'No Nazis.'

'No floods or thunderstorms or giant rats?'

'No.'

'No mad security chiefs who want to shoot us?'

'No – no Mars buggies and no Martians either,' said Tom. 'Just pigeons. Pigeons and Nelson – up there on his column where he belongs.'

Sarah opened her eyes and looked around. 'You mean we're really home?'

'That's right,' said Tom. 'We're really home.'

They hugged each other in relief.

'We're wearing our own clothes, too,' said Tom. 'The ones we were wearing when we left New York, all that time ago.'

'No time ago at all, I think,' said Sarah.

'How do you mean?'

'Transmat malfunctioned and shot us off to an alternate universe, right?'

'Three of them,' agreed Tom. 'Four, if you count the Napoleonic one, though we didn't stay there very long.'

He wondered how many other universes there were. What was it Sarah had said? Everything that can happen must happen, somewhere.

In theory, there were an infinite number of universes, one for every possible event.

'We weren't just travelling in other dimensions, we were travelling in time as well,' Sarah was saying. 'The Earth with the wrecked ecology and the Earth with the Mars Project were in some kind of future. When we came back to our own place, we came back to our own time as well. Hence the clothes!'

'If you say so,' agreed Tom. 'You're the scientist!' He thought for a moment. 'But look – if we've arrived back at the same time we went away . . .'

'Well?'

'Then none of those weird adventures really happened?'

'They did and they didn't,' said Sarah. 'You see, the thing about the parallel universe theory is . . .'

'I know,' said Tom. 'It explains certain interesting anomalies in particle physics – whatever that means!'

Sarah was still looking more than a little worried.

'Are you all right?' asked Tom.

'I suppose I just can't take it in, really.'

'Being home?'

She nodded. 'So much has happened.' She paused. 'Tom?'

'What is it?'

'I suppose we really are back in our own universe? Something ghastly isn't going to come round the corner at any moment? That really is Nelson up there on the column – not Julius Caesar or Genghis Khan?'

'I think the proof you need is on its way,' said Tom. He indicated two people hurrying towards them across the square.

His parents, Sarah's uncle and aunt.

What's more, they were their normal, everyday selves. His father, the tweedy, mildly scruffy university lecturer. His high-powered mother in her business-woman's trouser suit.

Tom and Sarah jumped up and went over to meet them.

Tom's father gave them a friendly nod, pleased to see them but too reserved to show it.

His more volatile mother hugged them and kissed them and told them off, all more or less at the same time.

'Where have you two been?' she scolded. 'Had you forgotten we were coming to meet you? You weren't there when we arrived at the transmat depot – we were quite worried. And now here you are, large as life! What happened to you?'

Tom and Sarah looked at each other.

'You first,' said Sarah.

'Well, Mum,' said Tom. 'As a matter of fact, we took a bit of a detour . . .'

*Suddenly a man in a black
uniform appeared, hurrying
down the corridor towards
them. He had heavy, brutal
features and he had a holstered
pistol at his belt. He was a
sinister, frightening figure and
Sarah saw that Tom was staring
at him in horrified disbelief.*

*'Oh no!' he whispered. 'It
can't be . . .'*

'Can't be what?'

'SS,' muttered Tom.

The year is 2015, and the transporter has malfunctioned,
reassembling Tom and Sarah in a parallel universe – one in
which the Nazis have won World War II. It's a world of
soldiers, guns and salutes, of work-camps and swift
executions. On the run from the SS and unable to trust
anyone, they must try to find a way back to their own
universe . . .

*"The action is satisfyingly frantic . . . (readers) will respond to
Dicks' punchy style and relish the neat twist teasingly placed at
the very end of the novel."* Books for Keeps

'Sarah!' Tom shouted as he clung to the flooded rubble. 'Sarah? Where are you?'

He tried to peer through the choking mists and gain his bearings in this strange, hostile landscape.

Tom and Sarah arrive in a parallel universe, many years from now, where disaster reigns. The planet has been ruined by man's pillaging and pollution. Cities are under water, virulent plagues have killed much of the population, genetically mutated crops have destroyed agriculture and giant rats roam the countryside.

Civilisation has collapsed and the survivors battle against each other. Tom and Sarah must use all their combined courage to survive and escape home before it is too late.

When Mr. 'hey, call me Dave'
Sissons suggests that 5B keep
a diary for a whole year,
reactions are decidedly mixed!
Yo! Diary! grants us exclusive
access to all areas of six very
different fifteen-year-old
minds:

Seb – the rebel and
'Spokesdood for a
generation';
Meera – a girl obsessed
with astrology;
Steven Stevens – so good
his parents named him twice;
Clare – the local neighbourhood Eco Warrior;
Mandy – Ms Personality and Karaoke Queen, and
Craig – convinced that he's the only virgin on the entire
planet.

Jonathan Meres has written a riveting and hilarious tale of
teenagers teetering on the edge of the millennium! It's a
story of changes, drama, love, intrigue and plenty of good
old angst! And that's just in the first week!

*"Meres' strong, irreverent characterisation and sharp humour
(he was a stand-up comedian with his own radio show) make
this a book that will achieve an effortless following."*
Publishing News

If you would like more information about
books available from Piccadilly Press and how
to order them, please contact us at:

Piccadilly Press Ltd.
5 Castle Road
London
NW1 8PR

Tel: 020 7267 4492
Fax: 020 7267 4493